SIR DALTON AND THE SHADOW HEART

CHUCK BLACK

MULTNOMAH
BOOKS

SIR DALTON AND THE SHADOW HEART
PUBLISHED BY MULTNOMAH BOOKS
12265 Oracle Boulevard, Suite 200
Colorado Springs, Colorado 80921

ISBN 978-1-60142-126-5
ISBN 978-1-60142-238-5 (electronic)

Published in the United States by WaterBrook Multnomah, an imprint of the Crown Publishing Group, a division of Random House Inc., New York.

Library of Congress Cataloging-in-Publication Data
Black, Chuck.
Sir Dalton and the shadow heart / Chuck Black. — 1st ed.
p. cm. — (The knights of Arrethtrae ; bk. 3)
Summary: While on a mission, Sir Dalton is captured by an evil Shadow Warrior, but even though he is bruised and beaten, he refuses to submit to his captor and initiates a daring escape that could lead to his death.
ISBN 978-1-60142-126-5
[1. Good and evil—Fiction. 2. Knights and knighthood—Fiction. 3. Christian life—Fiction. 4. Allegories.] I. Title.
PZ7.B528676Sg 2009
[Fic]—dc22

2009001120

Printed in the United States of America
2011

10 9 8 7 6 5

3/13

Praise for
Sir Dalton and the Shadow Heart

"With sanctified imagination, Chuck Black transports readers back to the days of chivalry and valor, clashing steel, and noble conflict—but ultimately he transports readers to the eternal triumph of the King who reigns!"

—DOUGLAS BOND, author of *Hold Fast in a Broken World* and *Guns of the Lion*

"Chuck Black is a word crafter who is able to weave Kingdom principles into the fabric of one's moral imagination. The characters he has created and the passions they exude will motivate readers to follow their examples, which have now been etched into their awakened conscience."

—MARK HAMBY, founder and president of Cornerstone Family Ministries and Lamplighter Publishing

"Chuck Black is the John Bunyan for our times! *Sir Kendrick and the Castle of Bel Lione* is a reminder of the origins of the spiritual warfare we are to fight daily."

—IACI FLANDERS, inductive Bible study teacher and homeschool mom

"Not since C. S. Lewis's Chronicles of Narnia have any fictional books boosted my faith so much. They make me cry with joy for what the King and the Prince do. They let me see our world through new eyes. I can't wait to read the Knights of Arrethtrae Series and experience more. The King reigns—and His Son!"

—SOPHIA, an avid reader

"I was so caught up in the books I would not do anything but read them. They were amazing…full of action, a little romance, and most of all, a love for the King and His Son. They made me feel as though I were truly traveling with the main character on his noble quest to spread the word of the King and His Son and standing in the middle of the Great Kingdom Across the Sea. I plan on reading the books over and over again. I loved the series so much!"

—ETHAN, an avid reader

SIR DALTON

AND THE SHADOW HEART

Also by Chuck Black

The Kingdom Series

Kingdom's Dawn (Book One)

Kingdom's Hope (Book Two)

Kingdom's Edge (Book Three)

Kingdom's Call (Book Four)

Kingdom's Quest (Book Five)

Kingdom's Reign (Book Six)

The Knights of Arrethtrae Series

Sir Kendrick and the Castle of Bel Lione (Book One)

Sir Bentley and Holbrook Court (Book Two)

I dedicate this book to all of the young men
and women who seek the truth of the Lord.
Be courageous, bold, and prepared,
and may your faith stand firm on the solid rock.

CONTENTS

Kingdom's Heart: An Introduction to the Knights of Arrethtrae 1

Prologue: The Shadow of a Heart 4

Chapter 1: The Piercing Shadow 5

Chapter 2: Newcomers 9

Chapter 3: The Seed 18

Chapter 4: The Qualm 24

Chapter 5: A Visit Home 31

Chapter 6: The Attack 36

Chapter 7: The Capture 43

Chapter 8: The Prison of Distazo 49

Chapter 9: A Desperate Plan 57

Chapter 10: Fleeing the Dark 63

Chapter 11: Return to Time 68

Chapter 12: The Mysterious Mister Sejus 72

Chapter 13: A Place of Beginnings 78

Chapter 14: Dividing the Code 87

Chapter 15: Sir Dalton, Knight of the Prince 91

Chapter 16: Back from the Dead 99

Chapter 17: Death Ravens 109

Chapter 18: The Sword and Its Knight 116

Chapter 19: A Warrior's Blade 121

Chapter 20: The Journey Home 128

Chapter 21: Love Lost 133

Epilogue: Standing Firm 139

Discussion Questions 140

Answers to Discussion Questions 148

"The Shadow Heart"
(written for *Sir Dalton and the Shadow Heart*) 158

Author Commentary 161

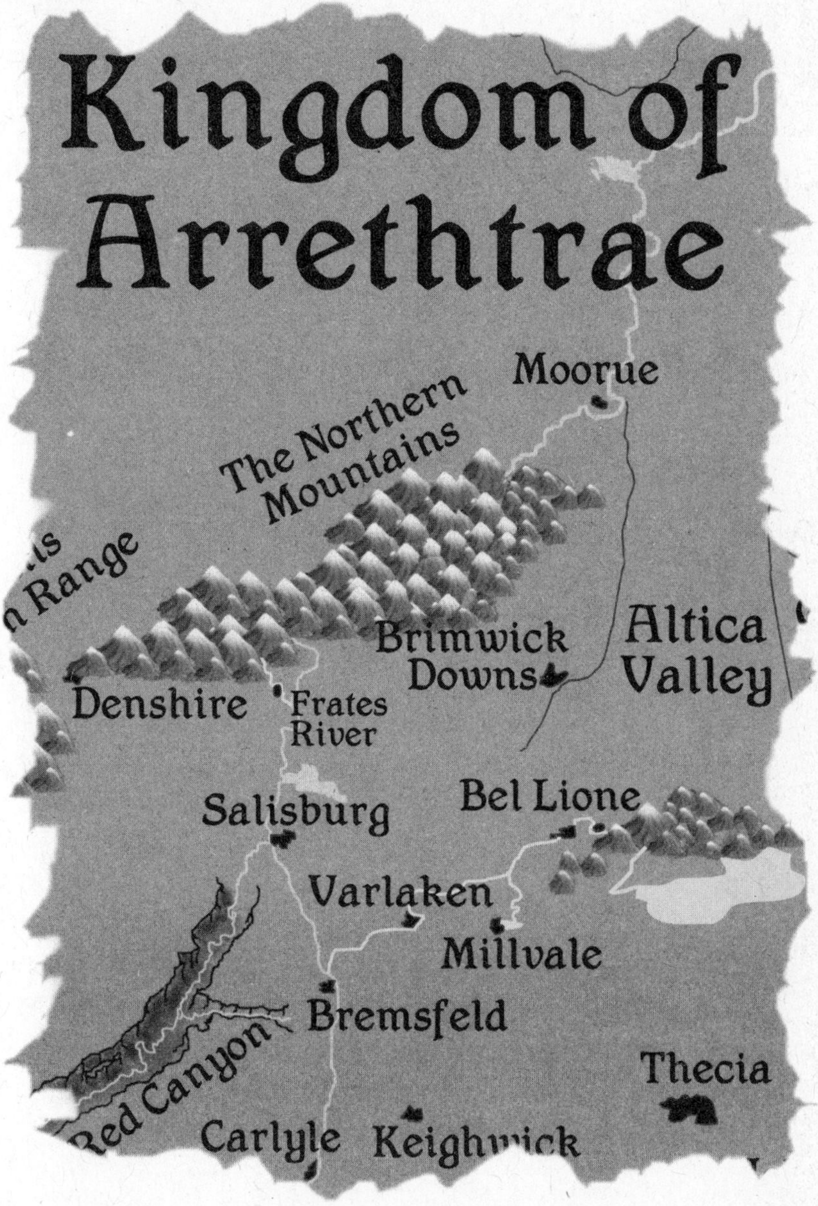

Kingdom of Arrethtrae

Moorue
The Northern Mountains
Range
Brimwick Downs
Altica Valley
Denshire
Frates River
Salisburg
Bel Lione
Varlaken
Millvale
Bremsfeld
Red Canyon
Thecia
Carlyle
Keighwick

KINGDOM'S HEART

An Introduction to the Knights of Arrethtrae

Like raindrops on a still summer's eve, the words of a story can oft fall grayly upon the ears of a disinterested soul. I am Cedric of Chessington, humble servant of the Prince, and should my inadequate telling of the tales of these brave knights e'er sound as such, know that it is I who have failed and not the gallant hearts of those of whom I write, for their journeys into darkened lands to save the lives of hopeless people deserve a legacy I could never aspire to pen with appropriate skill. These men and women of princely mettle risked their very lives and endured the pounding of countless battles to deliver the message of hope and life to the far reaches of the kingdom of Arrethtrae…even to those regions over which Lucius, the Dark Knight, had gained complete dominion through the strongholds of his Shadow Warriors.

What is this hope they bring? To tell it requires another story, much of it chronicled upon previous parchments, yet worthy of much retelling.

Listen then, to the tale of a great King who ruled the Kingdom Across the Sea, along with His Son and their gallant and mighty force of

Silent Warriors. A ruler of great power, justice, and mercy, this King sought to establish His rule in the land of Arrethtrae. To this end He chose a pure young man named Peyton and his wife, Dinan, to govern the land.

All was well in Arrethtrae until the rebellion…for there came a time when the King's first and most powerful Silent Warrior, Lucius by name, drew a third of the warriors with him in an attempt to overthrow the Kingdom Across the Sea. A great battle raged until finally the King's forces prevailed. Cast out of the kingdom—and consumed with hatred and revenge—Lucius now brought his rebellion to the land of Arrethtrae, overthrowing Peyton and Dinan and bringing great turmoil to the land.

But the King did not forget His people in Arrethtrae. He established the order of the Noble Knights to protect them until the day they would be delivered from the clutches of the Dark Knight. The great city of Chessington served as a tower of promise and hope in the darkened lands of Arrethtrae.

For many years and through great adversity, the Noble Knights persevered, waiting for the King's promised Deliverer.

Even the noblest of hearts can be corrupted, however, and long waiting can dim the brightest hope. Thus, through the years, the Noble Knights grew selfish and greedy. Worse, they forgot the very nature of their charge. For when the King sent His only Son, the Prince, to prepare His people for battle against Lucius, the Noble Knights knew Him not, nor did they heed His call to arms.

When He rebuked them for their selfish ways, they mocked and disregarded Him. When He began to train a force of commoners—for He was a true master of the sword—they plotted against Him. Then the Noble Knights, claiming to act in the great King's name, captured and killed His very own Son.

What a dark day that was! Lucius and his evil minions—the Shadow Warriors—reveled in this apparent victory.

But all was not lost. For when the hope of the kingdom seemed to vanish and the hearts of the humble despaired, the King used the power of the Life Spice to raise His Son from the dead.

This is a mysterious tale indeed, but a true one. For the Prince was seen by many before He returned to His Father across the Great Sea. And to those who loved and followed Him—myself among them—He left a promise and a charge.

Here then is the promise: that the Prince will come again to take all who believe in Him home to the Kingdom Across the Sea.

And this is the charge: that those who love Him must travel to the far reaches of the kingdom of Arrethtrae, tell all people of Him and His imminent return, and wage war against Lucius and his Shadow Warriors.

Thus we wait in expectation. And while we wait, we fight against evil and battle to save the souls of many from darkness.

We are the knights who live and die in loyal service to the King and the Prince. Though not perfect in our call to royal duty, we know the power of the Prince resonates in our swords, and the rubble of a thousand strongholds testifies to our strength of heart and soul.

There are many warriors in this land of Arrethtrae, many knights who serve many masters. But the knights of whom I write are my brothers and sisters, the Knights of the Prince.

They are mighty because they serve a mighty King and His Son.

They are...the Knights of Arrethtrae!

PROLOGUE

THE SHADOW OF A HEART

Some tales tell of gallant deeds done by men and women of might. Some tell of great battles fought to free the innocent from the tyranny of wicked men. But some tales tell of the journey of the heart, and such a one is this.

I am Cedric of Chessington, Knight of the Prince. I have taken upon myself the duty of chronicling the stories of many of my fellow knights... those living now and those who came before. Please do not think me overbold if I should implore you to pause in your own life's journey and sit with me these few moments. I have learned that pondering the life of another oft reveals both strengths and weaknesses in my own devotion to the King and his great Son. Such ponderings can beckon hearts to a nobler call and thus are worth every moment spent upon them.

Sir Dalton discovered an enemy lurking in the shadows of his heart—an enemy we must all face at some point. The Prince called one of his mightiest knights "greatest among all," and yet he too faced this enemy. Therefore judge not Sir Dalton, but glean from his tale the wisdom and the courage to let the light of the Prince so illumine your whole being until your heart holds no shadows at all.

Sir Dalton dared to look into the shadow of his heart... Shall we?

ONE

THE PIERCING SHADOW

Dalton dared not close his eyes, but he wanted to. He thought that perhaps if he closed them long enough he would awaken from this nightmare. His heart quickened, and his palms began to sweat. He tried to swallow, but his throat was so tight that the motion of his tongue stopped at the roof of his mouth and would not allow it.

"You fool!" The condescending words came from a dark, evil voice. "Did you really think you could escape me?"

Dalton stood before a true monster of a warrior. Lord Drox was a tower of muscle clad in black chain mail and gleaming black armor. He swung his gruesome blade from side to side as if to taunt Dalton. The warrior stood over seven-and-a-half feet tall, but to Dalton he seemed twice his own height. Dalton was facing a giant of evil and there was nowhere to run.

Dalton quickly loosened the dressing that bound his wounded left arm to his side. He gripped his sword tightly as Lord Drox swung his blade in an arced slice. The swords collided, and Dalton nearly lost his grip. Stunned by the power of Drox's cut, he fought the paralyzing fear that rose up within him.

Surely this will be the end of me.

He gripped his sword tighter and made a diagonal cut toward the hulking form in front of him, but Drox's blade easily met his blow. Dalton's sword vibrated as though he had struck a brick wall instead of an opposing sword.

Dalton recovered his position once more and held his sword before him. Drox actually lowered his sword and began to laugh. The warrior's deep chortles reverberated off the granite walls of the box-canyon arena where they fought. The canyon's walls rose high around them, and though Dalton had searched for an exit, he had found none. He thought of ducking into the trees or maneuvering behind some of the jagged granite outcroppings nearby, but such moves would be futile. There was no place to run.

Drox finished enjoying his moment of mirth and fixed Dalton with a look of leering hatred.

"Oh how I love to kill the incompetent Knights of the Prince!" He raised his sword and attacked again.

Dalton tried to stand firm and brought his sword to meet the first few cuts, but he quickly found himself in retreat. Drox's blade seemed to pound into Dalton's blade like the blows of a war hammer, and he could not sustain his defense. Drox brought a powerful two-handed horizontal cut from Dalton's right side.

Dalton gripped his own sword with both hands, hoping to withstand the impact, but the force of Drox's weapon sheared Dalton's sword in two and sent him stumbling backward. He flailed for a handhold to keep from falling, but there was nothing to grasp. Time seemed to slow as he fell to the ground and watched the upper portion of his blade fly end over end away from him. It landed in the dirt of the box-canyon floor just as his back hit the ground with a thud.

Dalton closed his eyes and hoped against reality that he would awaken from this nightmare. He saw the dark shadow over him through his closed eyelids and opened his eyes to see the evil form of Drox looming over him.

"Now you know who is truly lord of your life, knave. It is he who has the power to kill you." Drox's face twisted with utter loathing as he raised the hilt of his sword high above his head, the tip pointing downward toward Dalton. With both hands, Drox plunged the blade through Dalton's armored abdomen and deep into the ground beneath.

Dalton screamed against the steely invasion of his body as the fear of his imminent death fully gripped him. He released his grip on the worthless hilt of his broken sword and grasped the blade of Drox's weapon, convulsing in unbearable pain.

He wondered briefly why Drox had not pierced his heart instead. Then he understood. This warrior was so vile that he would draw even greater pleasure from executing a slow, painful death rather than a quick one.

Drox loosed his grip on the sword and knelt down beside Dalton. He looked into Dalton's eyes, clearly enjoying the fear, pain, and hopelessness he saw in them. His thin lips twisted into an evil grin.

"My pets prefer their meat fresh." Drox lifted his hand into the air, and a large raven with two wings on each side of its body landed on his wrist.

Caw! The eerie bird screeched as it looked down at Dalton with impenetrable black eyes.

"When you are too weak to fight them off, they will come," Drox said as he stood. "Knight of the Prince"—Drox spat—"He never cared about you, fool! You're just a dispensable pawn." He turned and walked away.

Pain saturated Dalton's body. The slightest movement amplified the agony tenfold. The sky above him filled with twenty hungry ravens, each one calling for others to join in the final torture.

One of the birds landed on the handle of Drox's sword, and the

movement from its landing nearly sent Dalton into unconsciousness. He screamed at the double-winged bird, but it showed no fear. Its feathers were sleek and glistening, its eyes as dark and evil as its master's.

Dalton knew he had but one faint chance—to lift the sword from the ground through his stomach and free himself. He grasped the blade tightly with both hands and took as deep a breath as he could, then pushed up against the embedded steel with all of his remaining strength.

The avalanche of pain crushed him into a semiconscious state, where his mind wallowed between the worlds of reality, memory, and dreams. The vision of a beautiful young woman filled his mind as he was taken back two years earlier.

"Lady Brynn…," he whispered, and reached to touch her…but she was not there.

TWO

NEWCOMERS

"Lady Brynn!" Dalton called out, and the beautiful young lass turned her head.

"Dalton!" she exclaimed and waited for him to catch up.

"Are you off to the haven?" he asked.

"Yes, the new trainer has arrived," Brynn said. She swiped a tousle of white blond hair from across her brow to reveal warm, deep blue eyes that seemed to capture Dalton every time he looked into them.

"I've heard." He fell in step beside her as they continued onward. "May I walk with you then?"

Brynn smiled and nodded.

It was early fall, and the kingdom seemed a glorious place of promise and adventure for Dalton. He was a young man who had everything going for him. Granted, he did not come from a wealthy family, but the kingdom seemed to be changing. When he joined the Knights of the Prince and began training with them, many of the social restrictions of his status seemed to fade. He had even been able to develop a friendship with Brynn, whose father was both wealthy and respected in the nearby city of Salisburg and the surrounding countryside. Dalton was grateful that her family had joined the Knights of the Prince too, for one day he hoped to pursue a more purposeful relationship with her.

"I hear he's a knight who just returned from a mission," Dalton said. "I wonder how long he'll be our trainer."

"I hope for a long while...if he's as good as the older knights say." Brynn smirked. "We've had four trainers in the last year and most of them weren't—"

Dalton held up his hand and nodded. "I know what you mean."

"We need someone who sees the kingdom as we do." Brynn gazed wistfully up into the patches of blue sky as they walked beneath the large sprawling oak trees that lined the roadway. "This is a time to live full, dream big, and enjoy life! We have the rest of our lives to live the dreary life most adults do."

Dalton watched her as she jumped onto a stump and raised her hands to her forehead as if straining to see the future. She was a slender, beautiful girl, and Dalton thought how fortunate he would be if her father would ever consider him as a possible suitor. He knew that he would have to prove himself worthy, and becoming an accomplished knight would certainly be a huge step toward that end.

Dalton had been born a commoner, the son of a blacksmith. Although he had begun learning the trade of his father, his heart had not been in it. His heart was exactly where Brynn's was, for he too yearned to live full and dream big. When he joined the Knights of the Prince, he had quickly won favor with the other trainees. The years of training as a blacksmith had developed a tight muscular frame. His friendly blue eyes, warm smile, and slightly dimpled chin were handsome features envied by most. He was a popular lad, and the others often looked to him for guidance. Older knights in the haven saw his leadership potential and often trusted him to give the other trainees direction while they attended to more important issues.

Brynn jumped down from the stump, grabbed his hand, and ran ahead, towing him behind.

"Come on," she said gleefully. "I'll race you to the haven!" She let loose and bolted ahead, turning to see if he would follow.

Dalton laughed and then joined in the sprint.

"This is Sir Dornan of Drearick," Sir Treffen announced as he stood before the thirty-two young trainees of Salisburg, some new recruits and others almost ready to be commissioned. "He will be conducting your training from now on. He's just returned from a mission, and I'm sure he'll be glad to tell you of it if you implore him to do so."

Sir Treffen lifted his hand toward the tall man with a tightly cropped goatee who came to stand beside him. Dornan seemed young for a trainer, and Dalton thought he must be either extremely skilled with the sword, or very wise, or both to be given charge over the training at the haven. Dornan nodded toward Treffen and then addressed the young knights.

"It is my extreme privilege and honor to assume responsibility for training you in service to the Prince. I consider this duty to you and to the other knights at the haven to be of the utmost importance."

The well-spoken introduction seemed to be exactly what Sir Treffen wanted to hear. He smiled and nodded as he stepped forward to address the trainees again.

"As each of you finish your training and embark on your own missions for the Prince, we will talk again. But for now Sir Dornan will be your source of instruction and guidance." He turned to Sir Dornan. "I'll be leaving now. Keep us informed."

"I will, sir," Dornan nodded.

The following day, two new recruits joined them at the training camp. Dalton thought them a bit strange. They seemed pleasant enough, but a little awkward—and much too serious for their young age. He guessed

Sir Koen was perhaps eighteen, his own age. Lady Carliss, Koen's sister, appeared about two years younger.

"Welcome to Salisburg." Dalton held out a hand. Koen looked at Dalton with skeptical eyes before taking his hand. His light brown hair was a little unkempt.

"This is Carliss." Koen gestured toward his sister. Her brown eyes stared straight into Dalton's. Something about them told Dalton that she viewed the kingdom differently than most youth. Her hair, nearly the same color as her brother's, hung to her shoulders in casual waves of inattention. The resemblance between her and Koen was unmistakable.

"Hello." She offered him her hand and gave him a small smile. A few of the other trainees broke from their groups and joined Dalton in the greeting.

"Where do you come from?" asked Makon.

"We used to farm east of Bremsfeld," Koen replied. "Things got tough there, and some of our kin have land near Salisburg, so..." He looked a little uneasy.

"Been training long?" Dalton asked.

At that, Koen's face lit up. "Since we were young—by our father."

"But you said your father was a farmer," one of the trainees said.

"Yes, but he knows the art of the sword," Carliss responded.

"Sir Orland often visited us on our farm and helped train us too," Koen added. "Do you know Sir Orland?"

Dalton shook his head and looked at his companions. The name seemed unknown among all of them.

"He came through our area some time ago and told us about the Prince," Koen said with enthusiasm. "Our whole family became Followers, and he helped train us with the sword." Koen glanced toward Carliss and allowed a slight smile to crease his lips. "We're excited to be part of the haven and continue training."

Three more trainees came to greet Koen. Dalton noticed that Carliss stepped aside and was soon left by herself. He looked over at Brynn, but she was deep in discussion with three other female trainees.

"Gather around, my young apprentices," Sir Dornan called to begin the day's lesson.

The trainees formed a semicircle around him. Dornan drew his sword and held it out. It was a magnificent weapon, a true work of art. Dalton glanced toward Koen and Carliss, and their eyes seemed to swallow up the sword with anticipation. Oddly, Dalton's heart stumbled slightly, and he was confused by his response. It was as if he had been thirsty for water but hadn't known it until he saw thirst in the faces of these newcomers.

"This is why you are here—to learn the art of the sword and to become trained Knights of the Prince." Dornan drew his sword in a wide, slow arc over the heads of the trainees and then quickly sheathed it.

"But you must first understand the kingdom and its people to be effective as a knight. There are many peoples, many cultures, many viewpoints, and we must adapt if we are to reach them and bring them freedom."

And so the daily instruction of the trainees began under the tutelage of Sir Dornan. He would lecture briefly on knighthood and then engage the trainees in dialogue on a variety of topics. Often the discourse would center upon an ethically challenging situation, with each trainee invited to voice an opinion. Dornan began to open their eyes to the many belief systems in the kingdom by sharing his own experiences. He spoke of his encounters with the nomads of Nan and also of the widely varying cultures now occupying the Kessons' Territory. Afterward, he would lead the trainees in a few skill exercises, usually involving horses and the lance, and the sessions always ended with food, drink, and song. But of the sword there was little training. All of the trainees were happy and content—or almost all.

♛ ♛ ♛

Three weeks later, Dalton once again joined Brynn on the roadway to the haven training camp.

"So what do you think of Sir Dornan?" Dalton asked.

Brynn shrugged. "He's certainly wise and experienced, and what he says is interesting. I'd say we're fortunate to have him."

"Yes, I suppose you're right," Dalton replied. "Everyone seems to like him, but the training seems..."

"Seems what?" Brynn prompted.

"Easy—or at least easier than before."

"What's so bad about that?" Brynn asked. "Who says it has to be hard? Besides," she said with a smile, "it's sure a lot more fun."

Dalton smiled back. "I guess you're right."

When they arrived, Sir Dornan was talking with a few of the younger trainees, and they all burst into laughter as he finished a quip. Soon they were all gathered about to begin their training.

Before Sir Dornan could address the trainees, Koen stepped forward.

"Sir Dornan, when do we begin seriously training with the sword?" he asked bluntly. "After all, we are knights, and that is perhaps the most important part of being a knight."

Dalton had noticed that Koen and Carliss both had become increasingly agitated with the training at the camp over the past week. Some of the trainees even began to tease them for being too stiff.

Dornan looked slightly perturbed and glared at Koen.

"Now that's an interesting thought," Dornan said whimsically. "How can you be a knight when you haven't completed your training, let alone had any experience? Seems a bit backward, don't you think? I myself trained for years before becoming a knight. Only then did I join the Knights of the Prince."

"But Sir Orland says that the ways of the Prince are different," Koen replied. "The Prince changed the order of the kingdom, so that we become knights as soon as we choose to follow Him; then we begin our training."

"Yes, well, the ways of the Prince have often been misrepresented in many instances. Wouldn't you agree?" Dornan said.

"Perhaps, but we have been given the example of Sir Gavenaugh and the Prince Himself on such things," Koen rebutted.

"Were you there?" Dornan asked with a wry smile. "Did you see this with your own eyes or hear it with your own ears?"

Koen's face turned red. "Well, no...but—"

"Listen, I am fully committed to all that the Prince taught," Dornan interrupted. "But life as a Knight of the Prince just isn't as simple as you seem to want to make it. You need to understand that the kingdom is vast and its people varied in how they will receive such new teachings. We must be creative in how we present the Prince and adjust our methods to accommodate the widely varying cultures that exist out there. I know; I've been there."

"But Sir Orland says that the Code—"

"I don't even know who this Orland fellow is. And as for the Code, it is clearly a guide, not a mandate. Besides, it was given so long ago—even before the Prince—that it is an antiquated document by now. Forcing the rest of the kingdom to live under such an archaic doctrine would never work. Our King is much more universal than that."

Koen scratched his head and looked exasperated.

"That is quite enough on that for today," Dornan said. "We shall postpone talk of the Code till tomorrow. I grow weary of your badgering, and you are quite the badger," Dornan teased.

"Yes, lighten up, Badger," one of the other trainees said. "Let us get to our training, for there's meat to be eaten and drink to be drunk."

"What training?" Carliss glared at the other trainee.

The assembly of young men and women fell silent. They looked at Sir Dornan. His nostrils flared and his jaw clenched. He then smiled condescendingly at Carliss and Koen.

"Very well," he said to Koen. "Draw your sword."

Koen slowly drew his sword, not quite sure what to expect. A number of the trainees snickered, for the sword was not a glamorous one, but Dalton noticed that the blade had been worked carefully to form a perfect edge.

Dornan motioned for everyone to back away as he and Koen faced off. Koen looked a bit nervous, but he took a swordsman's stance and did not cower.

"Mastering the sword begins with your feet. As you can see in young Koen's case, he could easily lose his balance with his stance so narrow."

Dornan attacked and put Koen in immediate retreat to make his point, and yet Dalton was impressed with how well the recruit handled his sword.

Dornan continued to speak as the sparring ensued. He was an extremely skilled swordsman. He maneuvered Koen at will until he executed a powerful bind and Koen's sword flew from his grip. Dornan held the tip of his sword at Koen's chest for a moment, then lowered it and smiled.

"Well you're certainly not ready to face a real enemy," Dornan said and slapped Koen on the back. "All of you draw your swords," he added. "Today we will work on stance."

An audible groan arose from the recruits, who had been looking forward to refreshments, and Dalton's friend, Sir Makon, whispered angrily to a trainee next to him. From that day forth, Koen and Carliss were ostracized. Koen became known as Badger, a nickname his sister seemed to despise more than he did. Her brown eyes would spark in resentment, though she said very little. She spent most of her time lurking quietly near the edge of the group of trainees.

Dalton himself didn't mind the two, though he wished they would make things easier on themselves by being a little more relaxed. He even made a few attempts to draw them into the social circle of the trainees... until Brynn made it quite clear that Koen, and especially Carliss, were not welcome. Dalton had to admit their gatherings were more pleasant without the tension and disapproval the brother and sister seemed to bring with them.

On two occasions, Koen's father came to observe the training. This seemed to annoy Sir Dornan in the extreme and served to further isolate Koen and Carliss from the rest of the trainees. Deep down, Dalton knew he should do something to make it better, but the animosity had grown too quickly and he didn't know how to oppose it. So he chose to ignore the problem as much as possible. His training was nearing its end soon anyway, and then it would be someone else's problem.

Why do they have to be so serious about it all? he asked himself as he walked home one evening. Dalton shook his head and set his mind back on his own future…and on Brynn.

THREE

THE SEED

Winters in Salisburg were typically mild, and this one was no exception. The crisp air in the evenings and the occasional frost in the mornings were easy to bear compared to the harsher cold that some had to endure near the mountains to the north.

Through the winter months, two trainees had been commissioned and were preparing for their next assignment. Sir Makon had chosen to embark on a mission for the Prince with an experienced knight, while another chose to remain in his family trade and support other knights on mission from home.

Soon it would be Dalton's turn, and he wrestled with his decision. Leaving meant leaving Brynn. But staying meant that he would probably never get away from the blacksmith trade of his family, and that too could end his chances with Brynn.

In the end, he realized there was only one choice. He had to leave her to win her...or rather to win her father's blessing.

One evening, during a training session, Sir Treffen rode into the camp with another knight Dalton had never seen before. Dalton was surprised when Koen and Carliss greeted the stranger enthusiastically, while Sir Treffen and Sir Dornan conferred for a time.

"Who do you suppose that is?" Brynn asked.

"I don't know." Dalton said. The stranger was a small man who hardly looked a knight. His head was nearly bald and, though trim and fit, he walked with a slight limp.

"Can't be anyone of importance if the Badger knows him," Brynn said.

Dalton didn't laugh, though a couple of the other trainees did. After a few moments, Sir Dornan gathered all the trainees, and Sir Treffen addressed them.

"Young knights," he began. "Sir Dornan tells me your training is going well. Each of you will soon be commissioned and given the opportunity to embark on a mission for the Prince. It is important that you understand that serving the Prince is a high calling. Whether you choose to serve here at Salisburg or venture into the kingdom on a mission is your choice. Though embarking on a mission may be more dangerous, both are equally important."

Sir Treffen motioned for the visiting knight to stand beside him.

"Today, I've asked a fellow Knight of the Prince from Vendenburg to brief you on some disturbing news. Sir Orland."

The visiting knight stepped forward and took a few moments to gaze into the eyes of each trainee. When he looked at Dalton, Dalton wanted to look away, but he didn't. For one brief moment, Dalton felt as though the man was looking for something within him but did not find it. His search went on, quickly scanning the rest of the trainees. His gaze ended with Koen and Carliss, but Dalton could not interpret the private message that passed between their eyes.

Sir Orland lifted his head and began to speak. "Serving the Prince is a noble and rewarding venture. But Sir Treffen speaks the truth: serving the Prince can be dangerous. If you've come to seek glory or fame or riches, you've come to the wrong order." Sir Orland paused. Dalton glanced about and knew that the man had already lost some of his audience.

"I have had the opportunity to travel to many havens in the region,"

Orland continued. "Havens much like yours, where we are training our young knights in the art of the sword. But something is amiss."

This seemed to regain everyone's full attention. Orland looked right at Dalton. "Some of our young commissioned knights are disappearing."

"What do you mean, sir?" Dalton asked.

"I have recently visited six havens in this region. More than twenty young knights cannot be accounted for."

"Are you certain they've disappeared?" Sir Dornan asked. "Or is it possible they are just delayed in their mission or have embarked on a different mission altogether?"

"It is possible," Orland replied, "but I fear something worse. And I suspect this is happening all across the kingdom. I am gathering information to make a report to Chessington." Orland looked again at the trainees. "You must remember that our enemy is dark and fierce and his minions are formidable. The Shadow Warriors will stop at nothing to destroy the cause of the Prince and His Followers!"

Dalton shifted from foot to foot. Sir Orland's passionate message made him distinctly uncomfortable, and he didn't know how to react to it. Should he be afraid, skeptical, nervous? Did this strange knight know what he was talking about? Dalton sensed the same discomfort from the rest of the trainees. Only Koen and Carliss seemed to fully embrace the warning. Their eyes were still fixed upon Sir Orland as they nodded their approval of his final words.

Sir Treffen stepped forward. "Take your training seriously, young knights." He and Sir Orland then mounted up and left.

Sir Dornan didn't seem overly concerned by Sir Orland's warning, and that sentiment was shared by nearly all the trainees. However, Dalton noticed that the evening's exercises with the sword lasted longer than usual. At one point, a break was called. While Dalton waited for the other trainees to take their fill of drink at the water bucket, he detoured into the forest trees to contemplate the warning of Sir Orland and his own impending decision.

Is there merit to Orland's warning? he wondered. When he considered the response from Sir Dornan and even Sir Treffen, he found it easier to dismiss Orland's words.

Caw! A raven called from a tree just two paces away. Startled, Dalton looked up. It was a huge bird, larger than any raven Dalton had seen, and its black eyes stared down emotionlessly from its perch. A bit unnerved, Dalton took a wide berth around the tree. The bird fluttered its wings, and chills went up and down Dalton's spine at what he saw. The raven was a freakish creature, for it had two sets of wings on each side of its body.

Dalton stared at it for a moment and then hurried on toward the water bucket. When he got there, a young lad filled a ladle and offered it to him.

"Thanks, sport," Dalton said trying to shake the willies from himself. He reached for the ladle. "Where are you from?"

"Nearby," the boy said with a crooked grin. His dark hair covered most of his ears and matched his brown eyes. "I've been watching you train some. What order of knights are you?"

"We're Knights of the Prince," Dalton replied.

"The Prince? Who's that?" the lad asked.

"He's the Son of the King."

The boy stood on his tiptoes to look at the other trainees who were gathering on the far side of the training grounds. "Which one is He?" the lad asked.

Dalton laughed. "He's not here. He lives in the Kingdom Across the Sea."

The boy scratched his head. "So why do you serve Him then?"

"Well, because He came here, and the Noble Knights of Chessington killed Him." Dalton flushed, realizing that his words sounded quite ridiculous.

The boy smirked and shook his head. "So you serve a guy in some fairyland who's dead. Sound's pretty far-fetched to me."

"It's not like that," Dalton said, trying to keep from sounding like a complete idiot in front of the boy.

"How do you know this Prince you serve was really the Son of the King?" The boy looked up at Dalton with eyes of defiance.

Dalton was at a loss as to how he could possibly explain the Prince to this contrary yet perceptive boy. He opened his mouth to speak but could think of nothing to say. *How do I know?* he asked himself. As simple as the question was, he had never really considered this before.

"Never mind," he finally blurted out.

"Okay." The lad held up the bucket for Dalton to refill his empty ladle.

Dalton huffed, then smiled and reached the ladle into the bucket. Just as he drew the water, the lad dropped the bucket, which smashed down onto Dalton's foot with a thud. The explosion of pain made him drop the ladle and collapse to the ground. Surely something must be broken to hurt this much. He cradled his foot and closed his eyes, trying to bear the pain until some of it dissipated.

"What's wrong?" Koen knelt beside Dalton.

Dalton tried to take a deep breath and squelch the throbbing with his mind.

"The boy dropped the bucket on my foot," Dalton said. He began removing his leather shoe.

"What boy?" Koen asked.

By now other trainees had gathered about, and Dalton was beginning to feel sheepish about the attention. He decided to leave his shoe on and brush off the pain, but it was nearly impossible. He looked toward where the boy was, but he was gone.

"You know," he said, "the boy who was here with the water bucket."

Koen looked confused.

"What happened, Dalton?" one of the trainees said. "Did you stub your toe?" He and four others laughed and walked away.

Koen reached out his hand, and Dalton took it. Koen lifted him to his feet.

"Thanks," Dalton said just as Brynn arrived. She looked at Koen.

"Sure," Koen replied and then left.

"Are you all right?" she asked.

Dalton forced a smile. "Of course," he said and took a step toward the training ground, then nearly collapsed again from the pain.

Brynn steadied him, and he put an arm around her shoulder for support. She helped him walk, but after a few steps he turned and looked back at the water bucket, which was lying on its side.

"What's wrong?" Brynn asked.

"Nothing." Dalton shrugged and turned back. Deep in the forest he heard the raspy *caw* of a large raven.

FOUR

THE QUALM

Dalton was commissioned in early spring with two other trainees. Sir Treffen put them under the mentorship of Sir Gulfar, a stout man with a voice that boomed like thunder. For the next three seasons, they traveled together to the havens at Bremsfeld, Carlyle, and Grisborn to further their training. During these visits, Dalton encountered other knights who were as intense about serving the Prince as Koen and Carliss seemed to be back in Salisburg. It was then that he further realized something in his own commitment to the order was missing.

He quickly learned to compensate for this apparent absence of knightly passion by mimicking the verbiage and skills of the other knights, and he found that his natural charisma benefited his efforts in the masquerade. What he could not do, however, was ascertain *why* he was struggling, and his times of solitary reflection increased. He tried to focus on his goal of one day winning Brynn, but even the memory of her beauty and their time together was not enough. Dalton even dared to ask of himself if he was a true Knight of the Prince.

One day, in his desperation to bring resolution to this internal conflict, he knelt before his sword of the Prince and repeated his vow of service. When he rose, however, it seemed that nothing had changed.

During his second year of training, Dalton was placed under the mentorship of Sir Putnam, and his travels in the kingdom broadened. Sir Putnam's particular mission was recruiting knights for the Prince. He was a skilled orator, and Dalton learned much from the man.

Another spring arrived, then warmed into summer. The two traveled to Millvale, where they were given the mission of helping start a new haven there. They were to help train new recruits as well as share the story of the Prince with the citizens of the village.

Shortly after they arrived, Putnam sent Dalton to the market for supplies and to acquaint himself with the town. He walked up a street full of carts and stands that advertised the wares of their owners. It was a delightful day, and Dalton enjoyed mixing with the throng of people at the market. He stopped and talked with many people, and the young maidens especially seemed to enjoy his attention. Eventually he stopped to look at a finely made shirt on a tailor's table.

"These are the finest shirts in all the town." A pretty young girl came to the opposite side of the table and lifted the sleeve of one of the garments. She smiled at Dalton and batted her eyes at him.

Dalton smiled back. "I'm sure they are, miss."

"Here," the girl grabbed Dalton's hand and pressed it to the sleeve of the shirt she was holding. "Feel the quality of the fabric, and look how tight the stitches are." The girl tilted her head slightly to the side.

"Indeed," Dalton said. "I do believe it is the finest I have ever seen. Is the work yours?"

"Partly, I hope to be as skilled as my father one day," she said with pride and motioned her head toward the shop behind her.

Dalton looked up and saw a man working in the tailor shop. Dalton realized that the girl had not let loose of his hand.

"The work is indeed impeccable, but I am more in need of a fine pair of boots," he said.

The girl's hazel eyes lost some of their sparkle. She took her hand from his and pointed up the street. "We have a friend who sells boots just up the street."

Dalton looked for the booth, but his eyes met the eyes of another man some thirty paces away. For a moment both men stared blankly at each other.

"Makon?" Dalton said in a hushed voice. "Excuse me, miss." Dalton began to walk toward the man. He was dressed not in the garb of a knight, but as an ordinary citizen. And there was no sword at his side, but Dalton was sure this was his friend from Salisburg.

"But sir, we have other clothing you might be interested in," the girl called after him, unable to hide her disappointment. "I would love to show you!"

Dalton did not really hear her. He quickened his pace, and the man who looked like Makon turned and bolted up the street. Confused by the response, Dalton began to run after him. When the man glanced back and saw that Dalton was pursuing him, his gait became a full sprint. Both men dodged people and stands as the chase ensued.

Once, Dalton nearly lost sight of Makon but happened to glance to his left and saw the leg of a man disappear down an alleyway. Dalton quickly made his way there and caught sight of the man disappearing around another corner.

"Makon!" he called out, but this only seemed to intensify their run.

Dalton's curiosity turned to frustration, and he became determined to catch this man no matter who he was. After a few more minutes, Dalton gained significantly, and it became apparent that there was no place Makon could go to get away from him. Dalton was now within ten paces and breathing hard. They had just turned up another alleyway when Dalton finally had enough.

He stopped. "Makon!" he shouted angrily.

At that the man stopped and slowly turned around. It was indeed his friend from training. Both men were breathing hard, and sweat flowed from their brows.

"What do you want?" Makon scowled between ragged breaths.

Dalton walked the remaining few paces and stood before his friend. "What...where...have you been?"

Makon took a deep breath and turned away. "That's none of your business," he snapped. "Just leave me alone."

Dalton stepped forward and put a hand on his friend's shoulder. "I can help you, whatever it is."

Makon quickly turned back and shoved Dalton's hand from his shoulder. He then grabbed Dalton's tunic with both hands and leaned in close to his face.

"No, you can't," he said with great pain in his eyes. "And no one can help you either." He leaned closer, his eyes filled with fear. "He'll come for you too." He glanced from side to side as if to see if someone was watching them. Then he pushed Dalton away.

"Have you completely abandoned the Code, Makon?" Dalton asked.

Makon snorted. "The Code is a farce, Dalton, written by some obscure person to lead the foolhardy on a wild chase."

To question the authenticity of the Code was to question the very essence of the order of the Knights of the Prince. Dalton was stunned by Makon's statement, and yet he could think of no reasonable or logical reply.

Makon leaned close to Dalton once more. "Leave me alone," he said in a quiet but fierce voice. He turned and ran up the alleyway. "Just leave me alone!" he shouted again as he disappeared at the next corner.

Dalton stood dumbfounded.

What has happened to him? he wondered. Why would Makon run from him, and why wouldn't he talk? It made no sense. Dalton remembered the warning that Sir Orland had given the trainees a year and a half earlier about Knights of the Prince disappearing. Was this what he meant?

Dalton walked back to the busy market street, but his mind was ever upon Makon and the few words he had spoken. The joy of the day had disappeared.

Two days later, the sun disappeared behind thick dark clouds that seemed as though they would stay forever. In spite of the dreary sky, Putnam and Dalton had managed to gather more than two hundred of the citizens of Millvale. Putnam spoke as Dalton mingled with the crowd, ready to answer questions from the people.

As Dalton heard Putnam speak the story of the Prince, he watched the people and marveled at the variety of responses. Some became angry, some scoffed, but others believed and grew joyful. Dalton thought about his own response to the story of the Prince and did not find it among the people.

Why do I feel so numb to these words that dramatically change the lives of people? he wondered. *I believe in the Prince and live the life of one of His knights. Tell me, my Prince…what am I missing?*

"That sounds like a pretty good story," a voice said from beside Dalton. He snapped his head to the right.

"But it's missing something," the young man said as he stroked his chin with his finger. He continued to stare at Putnam as he spoke to the people.

"What's that?" Dalton squinted at the man.

The man turned to look at Dalton with penetrating dark brown eyes.

"If the King and this Prince truly exist, why do they leave the kingdom in such a mess?" The young man paused for a moment to let Dalton think on his question.

Just as Dalton opened his mouth to speak, the man continued.

"For example, there are raids on the people, battles between castle lords, and starvation everywhere you look in the kingdom. If the King is so powerful, so wealthy, so good, then why has He let it go on for this long?"

Dalton scrutinized the man further. He was a broad-shouldered fellow with dark hair that hung to his neck. He was about Dalton's age and seemed far too intellectual for the rest of the crowd he was with.

"The King—," Dalton began, but was cut short.

"There can only be three possible answers," the man interjected. "Either the King and His Son don't exist, or they don't care about Arrethtrae, or they are too weak to do anything about what goes on. Whichever it is, only a fool or a man of ignorance would believe their story and follow them."

"That's not true," Dalton blurted. "The King and the Prince do exist! They do care and are very powerful!"

The young man leaned close to Dalton and pointed a finger at his nose. "How do you *know*?"

The question was simple and direct. But Dalton felt violated, as if this man had entered the room of his inner heart and vandalized the motivations of his soul. Dalton swallowed hard, and his mind froze in fear, as if a beast were stalking him and there was no place to hide. The man's eyes seemed to darken, and then he smiled.

"Believe whatever makes you happy, chap," he said and slapped Dalton on the back. "These people do." He swept his hand toward the crowd, then turned quickly to walk away. As he did, his scabbard swung swiftly about and sliced Dalton's thigh with a frayed edge of metal near the tip. Dalton winced in pain and covered the gash with his hand. Blood oozed through his fingers. Angry, he looked back up toward the man, but the crowd had swallowed him.

"Dalton, I need you, man," Putnam said as he came. "Where have you— What happened?"

"Nothing really," Dalton replied. "It's just a small cut…an accident."

"I'll get a cloth for you," Putnam replied, and went to his horse.

Caw! came the sound of a raven from the top of the tavern to Dalton's left. He looked and saw another strange, double-winged bird staring down at him.

Putnam returned with a bandage for Dalton's cut.

"Putnam, have you ever seen a raven like that before?" Dalton nodded toward the tavern's roof.

"Like what?" Putnam looked in the same direction, but the bird was gone.

"Never mind." Dalton muttered, continuing to stare at the rooftop.

Later, as Dalton thought about the encounter with the mysterious young man, he felt the presence of the beast once again, and it frightened him. He tried to put the incident from his mind, but the gash in his leg was a constant reminder. Only thoughts of Brynn seemed to help…at least for a while.

FIVE

A VISIT HOME

As Dalton's leg healed, the memory of the incident at Millvale faded. He made a trip back to Salisburg and was elated to see Brynn once again. To Dalton, she seemed more beautiful than ever, and his heart was all the more inclined toward her. He visited her numerous times at her estate. Her father seemed cool toward him but did not actually object to the visits. This encouraged Dalton significantly, but what fueled his heart even more was the delightful way in which Brynn responded to him.

"Your training is almost complete," Dalton said to Brynn as they walked beneath the sprawling oaks, enjoying the delightful sun of an unusually warm autumn. More than two years had passed since he had left home. "What will you do next?"

"I'm going to travel!" Brynn said with exuberance.

"On a mission then?"

"Not exactly," she replied. "I just want to see the kingdom."

"How's the haven? Sir Dornan still instructing?"

"Yes, but it's not been the same since you left."

"Koen still a thorn in his side?" Dalton asked with a grin.

"No, Badger was commissioned last spring and went on mission, but that pesky sister of his is worse than he is." Brynn smirked. "I'm surprised Sir Dornan even puts up with her."

Dalton looked ahead into the trees as he remembered Carliss's quiet intensity.

"She actually seems like a nice girl—perhaps too zealous for most people, but still..."

Brynn looked at Dalton as though he'd lost his mind.

"Nice? Are you kidding?" she said. "That girl had the audacity to confront Sir Dornan in front of the other trainees yesterday."

"Really? On what?" Dalton asked.

"Sir Dornan was explaining how he had seen such great chaos in the kingdom that it was logical to conclude that the King had removed his influence from the land and was really not involved in the affairs of the people anymore." Brynn hesitated. "It makes sense to me. After all, Sir Dornan has traveled to many regions and seen much more than we have."

Dalton had often wondered the same thing himself, and it did seem quite reasonable to think that way. "What did Carliss say?" he asked.

Brynn laughed. "She interrupted him and said that what he was teaching was not true. She got that strange, fierce look on her face, and she said the story of the Prince is evidence of the King's concern and compassion for the people. Or something like that."

Brynn grinned. "You should have seen Sir Dornan dismantle her argument. He's far too intelligent to be rattled by the ranting of a girl like Carliss." Brynn slowly shook her head. "You would think that brat would finally learn to be quiet."

"What exactly did he say?" Dalton asked.

"Well, he first asked her how many of the regions of the kingdom she had been to and then asked her to disprove him. Then he said that if the King did indeed establish Arrethtrae, it was more likely a result of discovery rather than establishment, and that the kingdom has been allowed to follow its own path of development for a long time. The King's hands-off approach allows the people freedom to explore life in many unique ways. He said that the Prince would agree. In fact, that's why he rebelled against the Noble Knights and their narrow-minded view of the kingdom."

They walked in silence for a moment as Dalton thought about Sir Dornan's words. Something disquieted his spirit after hearing Brynn speak of Sir Dornan, and yet how could one prove anything different?

They took a detour off the main road to the haven, one which they had traveled together a hundred times. The walk reminded Dalton of their earlier carefree days together, and he felt his uneasiness draining away. The arching tree branches billowed in the gentle breeze above them and soothed his mind with the rustling of leaves. How could he feel bad while walking with such a lovely companion?

"Brynn," Dalton looked at her. "I'll be on mission for another year or so, but I was wondering…"

Brynn looked at Dalton and smiled in a way that caused Dalton to want to reach out and take her hand.

"Yes?" she said.

"Well I was hoping that… You see, we've spent a lot of time together, and your father seems to be warming to me a bit."

"Yes?" Brynn's eyes seemed to drink in the beauty of nature and spill its splendor out every pore of her body.

"Would you—"

"Sir Dalton!" a cry came from the roadway ahead. The rider was at full gallop.

Dalton and Brynn broke from their enchanting walk to watch the rider approach. As he neared, Dalton recognized Sir Rolf, a knight he had trained with in Salisburg.

"Sir Dalton!" Sir Rolf called again.

Dalton lifted his hand into the air.

Sir Rolf reeled in his horse a few feet from them, and the animal seemed to protest the restraint.

"Yes, Sir Rolf," Dalton said. "What is it?"

"All of the commissioned knights are being called to the haven. We've just learned of a marauder attack on a small village not far from here. Where is your horse?"

"Just up the road at Lady Brynn's manor."

"Come, we must hurry," Sir Rolf offered a hand for Dalton to climb onto his own horse.

Dalton turned to Lady Brynn. "Will you be all right?"

Brynn looked sorely disappointed, but nodded. Dalton reached down, grabbed her hand, and kissed it. "I'll return quickly."

"Be careful, Dalton!" Brynn looked longingly at Dalton as he pulled himself up on the horse behind Sir Rolf.

Dalton had just enough time to wave, and then they bolted down the road. They quickly recovered Dalton's horse, Chaser, and soon were riding at full gallop to join with the other knights.

Dalton and Rolf joined the other commissioned knights at the haven and then rode for the village. It was not far, but by the time the contingent of thirty-two knights arrived, they were too late. Sir Treffen led the knights into the village, a village laden with sorrow and pain. The bodies of men and women lay in contorted positions on the ground. One woman was weeping over her dead husband. Sir Treffen dismounted and ran to her.

"Who did this, ma'am?"

"They took my children," she moaned as tears streaked down her cheeks.

"Where? Which way did they go?" Sir Treffen asked.

The woman pointed east toward the village of Felbridge.

"We will find them," Treffen said and mounted up.

As they neared the next village, Dalton began to hear cries of terror, and his heart raced. He had never truly faced an enemy before. Thus far, his entire life as a knight could be summarized mostly by the training camps he had attended and the havens he'd helped establish.

Sir Treffen drew his sword, and the other knights followed suit, fill-ing the air with the sound of impending battle. Their horses thundered onward, and Dalton's stomach rose up to his throat. They broke through the tree line and charged into a village in the throes of a savage attack. At once the marauders turned on the knights, and dozens of fights broke out in the village and the surrounding woods.

It took Dalton a moment to recover from his angst about the battle, but when he saw a vicious marauder strike a running woman from behind, his anger at injustice fueled his courage. He rode toward the marauder and soon found himself in a battle for his life. Dalton felt awkward fighting on horseback, and his adversary was much more adept than he. Dalton defended as best he could, but his enemy was able to land two hard blows that pounded into his chest and helmet. Dalton lunged at the man, and they tumbled off their horses.

Dalton fell on top of the marauder, cushioning his own fall and stunning the other man. He jumped to his feet and drew back his sword to cut through the dazed man on the ground.

Dalton hesitated as he contemplated the reality of his next action. He was about to take the life of another. His sword seemed frozen in place. The sounds of battle filled the trees around him, but he did not hear them, and he could not seem to move through this moment and into the next. He could just watch with fearful eyes as his enemy rose to his feet, a darkened smile crossing his face as he drew back his sword… and then stopped.

Six

THE ATTACK

"This one's mine." A fierce warrior had stepped in front of the marauder.

"Yes, my lord." The man stepped back and away, toward the rest of the fray.

This new enemy seemed strangely familiar. Dull black hair hung to his shoulders, and there was a small scar on his neck. He leered with thin lips, revealing yellow teeth.

"I've been waiting for you," he said.

The warrior's raspy voice rattled Dalton further. Fear mounted within him—fear that was also familiar, but much stronger this time. He stepped back and tried to recover himself, but he fumbled with his sword. He gripped it tighter and prepared for the fight, but felt awkward, as if he had never held a sword before.

"I am a Knight of the Prince," Dalton said to steady himself. "He is my strength."

"We shall see about that," the warrior said with another condescending leer. Then he attacked with a vengeance.

Dalton found himself in a terrifying fight for his life. The warrior was quick, powerful, and devious. Dalton had never faced such a foe, and his training seemed wholly inadequate for the task. His sword flew to meet a wide slice from the left, and he countered with a slice of his own. It was easily thwarted, and the warrior made a quick vertical counter that sliced through Dalton's tunic. The tip of the sword grazed his shoulder, but that was all.

Dalton recovered and tried to quicken the movement of his sword, but the warrior matched his speed, and Dalton knew his own skills were inferior. He heard the clash of the battle to his left and wondered if he could survive long enough for someone to come to his aid.

Movement caught Dalton's eye, and he chanced a quick glance to see two large ravens swooping toward him from the trees. He instinctively ducked just as the warrior executed a wide slice, and the diversion hindered his efforts to meet the slice. He managed to halt the enemy's blade, but its tip was now aimed at his heart.

The ruthless warrior thrust against Dalton's sword. Dalton pushed back against the blade of his adversary and moved it slightly, but the icy steel penetrated deep into his right shoulder. Dalton screamed and withdrew, but the warrior slammed another crosscut against Dalton's sword and it flew from his weakened hand. Gasping with pain, Dalton grasped his shoulder with his left hand.

The warrior held his blade at Dalton's chest, his face full of scorn.

"Where is the strength of your Prince now, knave?" the warrior chided. "There is only true strength in the steel of a blade, not in a foolish fairy tale."

Dalton looked up at the warrior and knew there was nothing he could do to stop the deathblow that was sure to follow. He knelt to the ground, weak and afraid.

"Have mercy," he pleaded.

The warrior began to laugh hideously. "Mercy? There is no place for mercy here, imbecile." He lifted his sword to cut Dalton through.

Thump! Dalton blinked as something flashed across his shoulder. The warrior screamed in fury and reached for the handle of a knife blade that was embedded in his right arm.

"Move, Dalton!" A voice came from behind him as the warrior tried to execute the interrupted cut.

Dalton fell to the ground and rolled away as the blade of the warrior passed just above him. That gave enough time for his ally to jump over him and bring his sword to the fight. The air was filled once again with the clash of swords as a fellow Knight of the Prince boldly stood between Dalton and his adversary warrior. Dalton could not see the knight's face, but he was intensely grateful for his presence.

He recovered himself enough to find his sword. He held it with both hands and stood to help his fellow knight, but there was no need. The warrior was in full retreat against the knight's mighty sword. A moment later the warrior fled the fight altogether.

"I'll be back for you, knave!" he called out in the distance.

Dalton shuddered.

"Thank you for saving my life, sir," Dalton said.

The knight turned around, and Dalton's jaw dropped.

"It is the Code, Dalton," the knight said. "To live for any other reason is vanity."

"Koen!" Dalton exclaimed.

Koen sheathed his sword to help Dalton, for his cut shoulder was bleeding badly.

"I didn't know you were here," Dalton said. He hadn't seen Koen for nearly two years, and something was different. Although Koen's facial features had lost the subtle remnants of boyhood and been replaced by the firmer lines of manhood, this was not the change Dalton saw. Koen seemed more mature and seasoned as a knight—far beyond Dalton.

"Sit here." Koen motioned for him to lean against a tree, and he set to bandaging Dalton's shoulder. "Our unit was called to the battle too," Koen replied. "I happened upon your fight by pure circumstance."

"You fought that warrior well," Dalton said.

Koen paused in his labor and looked at Dalton with a countenance of discernment.

"Thank you," he said with a quick nod.

Then Dalton realized that it was not only Koen who had changed, but he himself. Koen's serious resolve to serve the Prince had been ever present. But only now, after having experienced the reality of the kingdom battle, did Dalton see this resolve as a mark of true nobility and character rather than an awkward and foolish intensity.

Dalton was ashamed. Years earlier at the haven, Dalton had been the young man everyone looked up to. But here on the battlefield of life, Dalton was the one who looked up to Koen.

Koen finished the bandage and grasped Dalton's left hand, lifting him to his feet. Dalton held on to Koen's hand a moment longer.

"I owe you an apology, Koen."

Koen hesitated with his response again, unsure of what was coming. "For what?"

"For not befriending and defending you at Salisburg." Dalton dropped his gaze briefly and then looked straight at Koen. "I was wrong, and I'm sorry."

Koen's eyes narrowed, and he nodded. "I forgive you…friend."

Dalton grimaced, then smiled. "Friend."

Dalton helped Koen and the other knights tend to the wounded, but his strength quickly waned. When they prepared to leave, Dalton found it difficult even to mount his steed. Koen stayed close by him.

"Our farm is not far from here. I think you should rest there until you are stronger."

"Thanks, but it's not much farther to Salisburg," Dalton said. "I'll be all right."

After a few miles, however, Dalton was struggling to stay coherent, and he continued to weaken. He didn't resist Koen when they broke from the other knights and his friend brought him to his family farm.

Koen's mother removed Dalton's bandage and cleaned the wound. She tightly bound it up again with a fresh bandage. He fell onto a soft bed they had prepared for him and slept the rest of the day and on through the night.

Dalton awoke to the giggling sounds of a little girl with cheerful eyes and reddish blond hair.

"You sound funny," she said.

Dalton guessed he must have been snoring. It took him a moment to remember where he was and why a child might be standing next to him.

"Hi there—"

"Lacy!" a hushed but urgent voice called out.

"Uh-oh!" the little girl said. Her smiled vanished.

"Quick, hide on the other side of the bed," Dalton said with a wink.

The little girl grinned, eyes twinkling, and ran around the bed, kneeling down as the door opened. Carliss peeked into the room and realized that Dalton was awake.

"Oh...I'm sorry... I thought you were still... Lacy!" Carliss said, unsure whether to enter the room or go back outside and knock.

"Come in. I haven't seen any Lacy around here," Dalton said with a look of surprise.

A slight giggle escaped from the far side of the bed. Carliss opened the door wider and seemed at a loss.

"She wasn't supposed to disturb you," Carliss said. "Lacy! Out of the room."

A small head slowly rose up from behind the bed like a sunrise in the morning. The girl looked sheepishly at Carliss.

"Out," Carliss commanded.

The little girl's lower lip stuck out as she slowly made her way around the bed and toward the door.

"Goodbye, Lacy," Dalton called.

She turned to look at him, and Dalton winked. A smile creased her impish face, and she vanished behind the slender form of Carliss.

Dalton looked up at Carliss and was quite stunned by how much she had changed. Two years of maturity suited her well, something he hadn't expected. She was no longer a girl, but a striking young woman.

"Hi, Carliss." Dalton tried to sit up and winced at the pain that hit him with the movement.

"Are you all right?" Carliss hurried toward the bed. "Mother has gone to the neighbors and asked me to check on you."

The sheet fell from his shoulder to reveal his blood-soaked bandage.

"I've been better," he said, and grimaced a smile. He fell back to the bed.

Carliss inspected his shoulder more closely. "That bandage needs to be changed. I'll be right back."

Carliss returned a few moments later with water and a clean dressing and began to work on his wound. While she focused intently on her work, Dalton's gaze settled on her face. The process of cleaning was painful, and watching her brown eyes seemed to ease the pain. She glanced at him from time to time to gauge the level of discomfort her work was causing. When she was finished, she inspected her work and let a quick and subtle smile cross her lips.

"You ought to do that more often," Dalton said.

Carliss looked at him and furrowed her eyebrows. "Dress wounds?"

Dalton laughed. "No…smile."

Carliss blushed and busied herself cleaning up the mess of dirty bandages.

"Thanks, Carliss. You and your family have been so kind to me—something I don't deserve."

Carliss stopped and looked at him. "You're welcome. Are you hungry?"

"Starved!"

"I'll fetch some food and water for you."

"I'd be most grateful." Dalton watched her leave the room. *She doesn't seem like much of a brat to me,* he thought as he remembered Brynn's last comment about her. She was quiet and serious, but certainly not a brat. In fact, other than her zealous heart for the Prince, Dalton could think of nothing else about her that would cause the other trainees to ostracize her so.

It was a revelation that both disturbed him and encouraged him, and he wasn't sure why. He just knew that he liked being around this family.

SEVEN

THE CAPTURE

Dalton stayed with Koen's family for three days, until he was well enough to travel home to Salisburg. Koen rode with him to the haven but left within a week to rejoin his unit. Dalton stayed six weeks at the haven to allow his arm to fully heal. He enjoyed the reprieve from his travels, for it allowed him to spend time with Brynn. Her father was warming to him with each visit, and this pleased both Dalton and Brynn. She was commissioned during that time but had chosen to stay in Salisburg, so they were able to labor together when the subcouncil of knights at the haven needed them.

After his respite in Salisburg, Dalton was dispatched to Brimwick Downs on the edge of Altica Valley, where he was to enter an advanced training program. He was excited about this after having experienced his near-fatal defeat at the hands of a vicious warlord. That incident had etched the reality of the battle for the kingdom in his mind and fueled his resolve to become a true expert with the sword.

He said his farewells to Lady Brynn and her family and traveled northeast for two days, arriving in Brimwick Downs on a brisk fall morning. Much to his surprise, Koen was enrolled in the same advanced training class.

"Koen!" Dalton shouted as they arrived at their first session. "It's good to see you!"

Koen smiled broadly. "And you!" he replied.

"How have you been?"

"I've been well. How's that shoulder?" Koen nodded toward it.

Dalton grabbed the shoulder with his left hand and massaged it a bit. "Good as new, thanks to your mother and Carliss. Say, how is Carliss? I was at the haven three weeks ago when she was commissioned, but I haven't heard from her since."

"Carliss is well. She's now training under Sir Orland."

"Really?" Dalton asked. "Why Sir Orland? I didn't know the haven—"

"The haven doesn't," Koen interrupted. "My father arranged it just as he did for me." Koen hesitated. "He doesn't feel that the training at the haven is up to par, and Sir Orland is an incredible instructor. He's seen a lot of action."

Dalton thought about their training at Salisburg and agreed that he hadn't felt adequately prepared to face the warrior who had wounded him—at least not as prepared as Koen was.

"I'm looking forward to this," Dalton said as the trainer came to greet them.

"As am I," Koen replied.

Dalton thoroughly enjoyed his time in Brimwick Downs. The training was difficult compared to the training at Salisburg, and he came to enjoy the challenge of it. In the corner of his mind, however, something disquieted him. He marveled at Koen's commitment to the Prince, and the more he immersed himself in the training, the more elusive his own commitment became.

Somehow he felt there was a connection between his feelings and the incident with the warrior that nearly cost him his life. The next time he faced such a warrior, he would be ready…he told himself. And yet, as the weeks passed by, Dalton's concern about the incident with the warrior nearly disappeared from his mind.

His friendship with Koen strengthened, however. Their months together afforded time to forge a powerful bond of brotherhood between them. Dalton found strength in Koen's truly noble character and his steadfast commitment to the Prince. When the training at Brimwick Downs was complete, Dalton and Koen traveled back toward Salisburg together.

They arrived at Koen's farm east of Salisburg just before dusk, and Dalton took a few moments to greet Koen's family. He was pleased to see Carliss there and delighted to renew his acquaintance with little Lacy and the rest of Koen's siblings. But he lingered a bit too long. By the time he resumed his journey home, the receding daylight was obscured by dark, ominous thunderclouds. The wind howled through the trees, and Dalton quickened his pace to make it home before the rain came.

He took the shorter route through the woods south of Kaar Lake. Chaser, normally a steady animal, seemed unusually skittish. He spooked and turned about at the roar of thunder not far away.

"Easy, boy." Dalton patted the steed's neck. "Let's just get home before the real storm hits."

Dalton turned Chaser south again on the path through the woods but found it difficult to get the animal to move.

"Come on, Chaser. Let's go," he said firmly.

Caw! A black mass swooped down at Chaser's head, and the horse reared up in fear, throwing Dalton from the saddle. He hit the ground with a *thud* that seemed to jar his spine up into his skull. Chaser bolted back up the trail from which they had come, away from the approaching storm.

Dalton would have been angry, but something deep in his soul evoked a different emotion. He stood and looked down the road at the fleeing animal.

"Chaser!" he yelled, but the howling wind stifled his voice, and the horse disappeared into the blackness of the forest trees. Thunder cracked through the sky, and intense lightning illuminated the forest walls in brilliant, brief flashes.

Dalton's anxiety intensified as he remembered the black raven that had spooked his horse. Chills crawled up and down his spine as he sensed an ominous presence behind him. Was it just his imagination? He slowly turned about, half expecting to see some nightmarish figure, then breathed a sigh of relief when the road before him was empty.

Crack! Thunder exploded simultaneously with a lightning strike just a short distance to his left, and the forest flashed with a burst of bright white light. Dalton froze in fear, for in that instant his eyes beheld the image of his nightmares. Though the appearance was brief, it was engraved in his mind forever. A towering, dark armored warrior stood just two paces away with a wicked sword drawn, ready to cut Dalton in two.

Dalton drew his sword in an instant and executed a powerful slice toward the position where he had seen the warrior. His sword flew through the air in a full circle, severing only the wind that howled there. Dalton's fear gripped him and swallowed him whole, for this beastly warrior was someone from his past, he instinctively knew. He moved from his position and tried to listen for his enemy, but it was useless.

Another bolt of lightning flashed, and this time Dalton's eyes widened in horror as he caught a glimpse of the massive warrior finishing a two-handed slice aimed for his left shoulder. The impact was unavoidable, and there was nothing he could do but gasp.

The blade slammed into his upper arm with the force of a battle-ax. Though his chain mail buffered his skin from the sharp edge of the blade, he felt his bone crack beneath the impact. The force of the blow carried onward and slammed Dalton into a tree, his head careening into the trunk with a thud.

Dalton collapsed to the forest floor like a rag doll, nauseated from the pain in his arm and head. He curled up and tried to cradle his left arm, but a massive hand encircled his throat and dragged him a few feet farther into the trees. When he attempted to roll away and make a run for it, a massive boot crushed him to the ground.

Deep, guttural laughter overpowered the sound of the wind, and the lightning flashed once again. Dalton caught another glimpse of his beastly adversary, his boot pressing against Dalton's chest like a massive boulder and his dark sword pointing at Dalton's throat. Black stringy hair swished about the warrior's shoulders in the wind. Dalton gaped, for this warrior looked much like the one who had nearly killed him months earlier, only much larger now. The scar on his neck was too much to be coincidence, and Dalton trembled in fear. Surely he was facing none other than one of Lucius's powerful Shadow Warriors.

How is this possible?

"I told you I would come back for you, knave." The warrior sheathed his sword, drew his knife, and knelt down close to Dalton. "I always come back!"

Dalton cowered in the face of the warrior's overpowering strength and knew his death was imminent. Lightning now illuminated the forest in bright flashes every few seconds, giving Dalton frequent images of his impending demise. The first drops of rain hit his face and mixed with the blood that oozed from his forehead. His arm lay limply at his side.

"Who are you?" Dalton said weakly.

Lightning flashed, and the warrior was now only inches from Dalton's face. His knife momentarily gleamed near Dalton's right eye. The warrior's eyes were deep and black. He was so massive that Dalton felt like a child in his hands.

"I am Skia Ek Distazo, but you will call me Lord Drox. I have been with you from the very beginning, my ignorant young fool."

"Dalton!" a faint voice called through the wind, rain, and trees.

"Koe—" Dalton tried to call back, but Drox's massive hand pressed hard against his mouth and cut his plea short.

The warrior dragged Dalton farther into the woods and behind a large tree, where they could just see the road a few paces away. He tightened his suffocating grip on Dalton's face and pressed the knife against his throat.

"Cry out, and it will be your last!" the evil voice whispered in his ear.

"Dalton!" Koen's voice was unmistakable now. He passed by them on the road, leading Chaser behind him.

Dalton dared not move, but he was amazed that this warrior was hiding from Koen at all. Drox was so huge and so powerful that surely he could kill Koen with as much ease as he had defeated Dalton. And yet Dalton sensed apprehension in Drox's grip.

"Dalton!" Koen's voice was nearly imperceptible now.

The rain became heavy sheets of water that drenched Dalton and added to his misery, for only a miniscule amount of air was passing between Drox's fingers and into Dalton's nostrils. He struggled for each breath, and the water nearly closed off his precious air.

Just when he thought he would pass out, Drox dropped his hand from Dalton's mouth and lifted him to his feet. Still a prisoner of the powerful grip, Dalton was dragged to Drox's horse. His hands and feet were bound, his broken arm screaming in protest. A dirty rag served as a gag, and a hood was placed over his head. Then he was thrown facedown behind the horse's saddle.

Drox mounted and steered his horse deeper into the forest, away from the road. With every strike of the horse's hooves, pain exploded through Dalton's body, and he screamed into his gag. Finally he could take it no more. Dalton sagged into unconsciousness on his journey of woe.

EIGHT

THE PRISON OF DISTAZO

Dalton faded in and out of consciousness as the Shadow Warrior took him deeper into the forest. To Dalton, it seemed they had traveled for an eternity. At one point he heard other dark voices and roused to a sketchy consciousness. Drox dismounted, and no matter their destination, Dalton hoped that this was the end of their travels.

Dalton heard the snorting and pawing of many horses nearby.

"Rise up, Distazo," he heard the voice of another powerful warrior say. "What manner of prisoner have you captured for me this time?"

"He is another young fool from the city of Salisburg, my lord. I've been working on him and many others for years."

"Ah, I am pleased with your work. Which of my deceptions worked best with him?"

"He believed a little of all of them, my lord. Just enough to make him weak and vulnerable."

"Good...good. That is always the most effective. And are you training more Vincero Knights?" the dark lord asked. The mere sound of his voice made Dalton shudder. If Drox was this dark lord's servant, Dalton was glad he could not see an even darker face of evil.

"Continually, my lord. Before long, the havens won't even recognize them."

The dark lord laughed loudly, and other grim chortles joined him.

"Carry on, Distazo. One day I will come and visit your prison myself."

"I would be honored, my lord," Drox said. Minutes later he mounted up once again.

Dalton heard the sound of many horses galloping away. Then Drox moved onward, and Dalton once more fell into the blackness of his mind.

Dalton opened his eyes to a place of utter despair. He was lying in a heap on the floor of a dank, filthy prison cell. He moved to sit up and then screamed in agony against the pain that exploded from his left arm. He waited for the intensity of the pain to subside before trying to move again. This time he carefully cradled his arm with his right hand and then moved to sit up. Even then, the pain was nearly unbearable.

He took a deep breath and rested against the stone wall at the back of the cell. The throbbing in his head added to his misery. He took another breath and looked around. Only now did he realize that there was no door to his prison cell. At the front of the cell there were bars, but the door had been removed. The way stood open.

A prison cell with no door? How strange!

"Where am I?" he gasped into the blackness.

"You are in Drox's prison," a voice answered gently.

Startled, Dalton looked to his right to see a man a few years older than himself. Dressed in the garb of a knight, he sat on his haunches, staring at him through the iron bars from the adjacent cell. His tunic was dirty and worn, his chain mail rusty. From the man's accent, Dalton guessed he was from the far northern region of the kingdom.

"Who are—"

"Shh!" The man held his finger to his lips and pointed toward the front of the prison cells.

Dalton made a monumental effort to scoot a few feet to the man and leaned against the bars next to him.

"Who are you?" he whispered.

"I am Si Kon. But my name is of no significance here. I am…was… just like you. A Knight of—"

The man stopped short and looked at Dalton with fear in his eyes.

"You mean a Knight of the—?" Before Dalton could finish, the man reached through the iron bars and slapped his hand over Dalton's mouth. He held it there tightly as he slowly shook his head, his eyes wide.

"Do not speak that name here," he whispered, then slowly removed his hand.

Dalton looked left and right and could see many cells each way. As near as he could tell, all were occupied.

"Why don't the cells have doors on them?" he asked softly. "Is there an outer chamber that is locked?"

"No," the knight replied. "There is no outer chamber, and the passageway out of the prison is not guarded."

Dalton was confused. "Then why don't you and everyone else here leave?"

"Because I"—Drox's dark voice echoed through the prison cells—"will stalk you, hunt you, and utterly destroy you!" The warrior stooped to enter Dalton's cell. Si Kon scuttled away to the far corner of his own cell and watched in horror. Fear swept over Dalton again as this beast of a warrior strode over to him.

"You begged for mercy once before, and now I offer it." Drox's smile managed to be both terrifying and enticing. "Renounce your foolish beliefs, and you are free to go. Many have done so, and it is a simple thing, especially since you don't really believe all that nonsense about the Prince anyway…yes?"

Dalton's mind raced through the possible outcomes of Drox's apparent trickery. Could it be that simple? Is this all the massive warrior truly desired, for Dalton to renounce the Prince? Dalton considered it carefully, but deep in the center of his heart, something would not let his lips form those words. Every fiber of his body ached to be free, no matter the cost, and the pain in his arm and head screamed against his defiance, but still Dalton resisted.

"No," he said quietly.

Si Kon looked away as the wrath of Drox erupted in a vile string of curses. He reached down and grabbed Dalton's upper arms with his huge hands. Dalton screamed as new agony shot through his broken left arm.

Drox lifted him into the air and shook him. "You will, fool. One day you will—and I will revel in that day!"

Drox threw Dalton into the corner of his cell and left. Dalton's mind wallowed on the fringe of consciousness, for the pain took his breath away. A few moments later, Si Kon entered Dalton's cell with some cloth and two flat pieces of wood.

"You are brave," he said as he gently helped Dalton sit up again. "Perhaps foolish like the rest of us, but brave nevertheless."

Si Kon set to splinting Dalton's arm with the wood and the cloth. The process was incredibly difficult to bear, but once it was complete, Dalton felt mildly better. They fashioned a sling from Dalton's belt, which helped immensely.

"Thank you," Dalton said.

Si Kon nodded.

"How long have you been here?"

"Many, many months," Si Kon said sadly. "I miss my wife and two daughters."

"Have you ever considered escape?" Dalton asked.

"At first, every day. But now..." His voice trailed off. "Some have tried, and they were killed. It is our fear of Drox that imprisons us, not the iron bars."

With Si Kon's help, Dalton stood and walked to the front of his cell. The prison was inside a massive underground cavern. An open area in the center was surrounded by hundreds of cells just like Dalton's. Some had iron bars, but some were just alcoves in the granite walls. The walls and ceiling were grungy and black. The ceiling rose in a jagged arc from the cells to a height of thirty to forty feet. At the top, Dalton saw birds flying in and out of a ragged opening that must have led to the outside world. A steady stream of water dripped from the entrance and fell to a mucky pool below. Torches set in sconces along the walls illumined this morbid prison.

To his left, Dalton could see the main entrance of the cave—a dark tunnel. On the far right, four lean and vicious canines were devouring the carrion of some creature. Their hairless hides were covered with large blotches, and the largest was the size of a small bear.

Not far from the hounds was a large, jumbled stash of swords. Dalton looked at Si Kon and then motioned toward the weapons.

"Drox calls them his hounds of despair," Si Kon said with a smirk.

"Not the dogs," Dalton said. "The swords."

"They are ours."

"But they are practically unguarded," Dalton said with surprise. "There are many knights here, and only one Drox."

"Drox is as powerful as a hundred knights," Si Kon said. "We would be fools to try...dead fools."

Dalton was stunned by his response and marveled at the apparent power Drox possessed over the minds of their fellow knights. Then he realized that he too was Drox's prisoner and dared not condemn his brothers and sisters just yet.

"Besides," Si Kon continued, "there are the hounds, the death ravens, the guards, and Drox's Vincero Knights. They will do little to stop you from leaving, but once outside you will be hunted again. Hunted by them like sport. And if they don't get you, Drox will. Then when he finds you…" Si Kon's gaze dropped to the floor. "It is hopeless to try."

"This shouldn't be," Dalton said in exasperation. "We are Knights of the Prince!"

"No!" Si Kon said. "I told you. You cannot speak that name here!" He slowly backed away from the cell opening as a sinister growl sounded.

The hounds had all stopped their feast. They looked Dalton's direction and lurched to their feet. The largest ran toward his cell, and the other three followed close behind. Now Dalton wished his cell had a door, for there was nothing to stop them. He backed away as the hounds approached the cell opening. All four snarled viciously, revealing yellow, bloodstained fangs.

"If they attack, give them your good arm," Si Kon said in a hushed tone. "The chain mail will help."

The pack leader lunged for Dalton's neck, and he raised his right arm just in time for the hound to clamp its jaws down on his chain mail. It held, but the force of the hound's bite was powerful. Another hound attacked, and Si Kon intercepted it with his own arm. The other two hounds guarded the cell opening as if to keep their prey from escaping.

Dalton felt the teeth of the hound pierce his flesh, though not deeply. The animal growled and yanked backward, opening the wounds further. Dalton knew his arm would be a mangled mass of torn flesh were it not for his chain mail.

The hound released its grip and poised for another attack. Dalton heard Si Kon fighting with the second hound.

"Release!" a voice commanded from just outside the cell.

The four hounds ended their attack and slunk away from the cell. A knight in black armor stood at the cell opening. He crossed his arms and glared at Dalton.

"Si Kon, you should know better than to join yourself to fresh meat."

Si Kon scowled at the knight as he cradled his arm.

"Back to your own cell," the knight commanded.

Si Kon went to the opening of his own cell, and the knight shoved him from behind. "Keep quiet!" Then he moved away.

Si Kon went to the iron bars between their cells and sat down. Dalton leaned against the bars close to him.

"I'm sorry," Dalton whispered as he took a deep breath. "I didn't know."

"I will die before I become one of them," Si Kon murmured.

"What do you mean?" Dalton massaged his arm with his left hand, thankful the attack of the hound had left only minor cuts.

Si Kon turned and looked at Dalton with narrow eyes. His straight black hair had grown so long that it nearly covered his eyes.

"He was once one of us, but Drox turned him into a Vincero Knight." The disgust in Si Kon's voice was evident.

"I didn't think such a thing was possible," Dalton exclaimed. He couldn't imagine a fellow knight ever serving someone as evil and loathsome as Drox, especially after having come to the knowledge and enlightenment of the Prince.

"Nor did I, till I was brought here," Si Kon said contemplatively. "Perhaps those who turn never truly served the Prince."

At that, Dalton's head dropped slightly, as did his heart. *Do* I *truly serve the Prince?* he wondered. Was there some purpose or consequence for what he was enduring, or was it all simply a matter of circumstance? Drox's very presence seemed to indicate something more—or something less in Dalton and his service to the Prince.

"I know your thoughts," Si Kon said quietly. "I've lived with them for two years now. Unfortunately I have no answer for you."

"Then I will find my own...when I leave this wretched place," Dalton said, finding a source of resolve that surprised him. "When my arm is whole, I *will* leave."

Si Kon gave a quick huff. "Everyone who comes here is injured in some way. Drox makes sure of it. By the time your arm is healed, your heart will be sick. It is his way, and it always works." Si Kon lay down on the stone floor and closed his eyes. "I am sorry, my friend. Drox is too strong, and you will never leave—never."

NINE

A DESPERATE PLAN

In Drox's prison there was no day or night, just work time and sleep time. The sun and moon were never seen, and thus the only distinction between day and night was when half of the torches were extinguished for the sleep period. For all Dalton knew, they might be laboring at night and sleeping in the middle of the day. He tried to keep track of the passing time by scratching a mark for each sleep cycle in the corner of his cell.

The prisoners were all given tasks to keep them occupied during waking hours. Some tasks were necessary to the survival of the prisoners, while others were simply menial and often meaningless.

Over the next four weeks or so, Dalton thought often about Si Kon's words. They scared him and angered him at the same time. He daily resolved to keep the thought of escape foremost on his mind, biding his time while his arm healed.

Dalton learned that all of the prisoners were followers of the Prince, both men and women, and most were young like him. The older prisoners seemed like hollow shells, and they never talked. They simply did their duties, ate their meals, and fell asleep to repeat the next day.

The prisoners were frequently threatened and beaten at the slightest infraction of Lord Drox's prison rules—all but the older ones, who always did what they were told. The prisoners were discouraged from talking among themselves and thus developing any camaraderie or unity. The Vincero Knights, the guards, the hounds, and Drox himself enforced this rule with special vigor.

And at the end of each day of labor, Drox would stand in the middle of the open chamber. His voice boomed throughout the prison cavern.

"There is no King. There is no Prince!"

A dozen or so guards and a half-dozen Vincero Knights stood about the cells and replied, "There is no King. There is no Prince!"

"Arrethtrae belongs to the strong, and only fools follow the Code!"

"Arrethtrae belongs to the strong, and only fools follow the Code!" the Vinceros echoed.

"Let he who is strong and not a fool come forth and profess these truths, and I will set him free." Drox would then wait for any prisoner to step forth from his cell.

One time Dalton saw a fellow knight step forward. The entire cavern fell to absolute silence as the man walked with slumped shoulders to stand before Drox. Dalton wanted to scream out to stop the man, but fear of retribution stayed his tongue.

"What are the truths you have learned here and will now live by?" Drox asked.

"There is no King. There is no Prince," the knight muttered.

"Speak loudly for all of the foolish to hear," Drox demanded.

"There is no King. There is no Prince! Arrethtrae belongs to the strong, and only fools follow the Code," the man said loudly.

Drox gave him a malevolent grin.

"You are free to go." Drox motioned toward one of the Vincero Knights, who stepped forward with a black hood in his hand to escort the prisoner out.

"See how simple it is?" Drox bellowed. "A few simple words, and all of your misery ends. You needn't even renounce your oath as a knight. Simply profess one or two of these truths, and you will be free!"

Dalton learned from Si Kon that often when one knight came forward, two or three others would follow. He also learned that Drox would offer to train a freed prisoner into a Vincero Knight if he sensed true disdain for the cause of the Prince and if the prisoner would fully renounce his oath to the Prince. This happened rarely, but it did happen, and these retrained knights became some of the fiercest Vinceros of the kingdom.

That night Dalton lay awake long into the sleep hours in spite of his fatigue. The image of the defeated knight uttering those words replayed over and over in his mind. Dalton ached for freedom too, and for just one brief moment he wondered if it would be so bad to follow in the prisoner's footsteps. He imagined being back in the kingdom, a free man with no duty to *anyone*...back with Lady Brynn.

It was then that Dalton's thoughts came to the incident with Makon in Millvale. *Makon must have been here and gone forward just like the knight earlier today,* Dalton thought. He remembered the look of fear in his friend's eyes and realized that Makon had not been free at all. He was still a prisoner to the fear of Drox and would be all of his days.

Dalton grew angry with himself as he realized his thoughts were beginning to change, just as Si Kon had said. A fire rose up in his bosom, and he extinguished the thoughts of apathy and compromise that tugged on his mind.

"Si Kon," he whispered. "Si Kon!"

Dalton heard his friend stir.

"Si Kon, come close."

Si Kon moaned and crawled to Dalton.

"What is it?" he asked annoyed.

"Tomorrow I am leaving," Dalton whispered so quietly into Si Kon's ear that virtually no sound passed his lips.

"But your arm is not fully healed yet," Si Kon protested.

"I cannot wait. I must go now," Dalton paused. "Come with me, my friend. With two of us, we will have a better chance."

Si Kon was silent, and Dalton wondered if he had fallen back asleep.

"We will die, Dalton. Drox will surely find us and kill us. I'm sorry… I cannot."

"Then help me," Dalton pleaded, "and I will come back for you with an army to set our brothers and sisters free."

After another long period of silence, Si Kon spoke. "You will need a sword. Tomorrow at labor's end, I will create a diversion. It will be up to you to recover a sword and hide it in the nearest cell—Lim's cell. I believe he will take the risk for us. At midsleep, the sword will pass through the cells to you. After that, you are on your own. The exit to the cavern becomes a tunnel that leads upward. Beyond that, I do not know what you will find. No one knows where in the kingdom this wretched place is. We could be in the Wastelands, for all I know."

"Thank you, Si Kon," Dalton said. He asked his fellow prisoner many more questions until he was satisfied that he knew as much as possible about the prison and those who guarded it. His mind raced long after their conversation until he finally relinquished himself to a final few moments of restless sleep.

The following day, Dalton could think of nothing but making his escape. He had moments of great anxiety as he thought of facing the dangers, but he quelled them and firmly set his heart to the task. He remembered Si Kon saying that exiting the prison might not be that hard. Perhaps with a sword he would have a chance. He decided that everything hinged on his success in acquiring a sword.

The end of the labor time was approaching. Dalton carried a bucket of water toward the cells nearest the pile of swords…and the hounds of despair. Si Kon was working on the far side of the chamber carrying rocks from one pile to another. He glanced toward Dalton as he passed by a guard. Just then he dropped a rock on the guard's foot. The guard howled in pain, dancing in a circle and cursing him.

"Fool!" a Vincero knight yelled and rushed over, drawing his sword to strike Si Kon.

"I'm sorry, my lord." Si Kon lowered himself to the ground. He had all of the attention of the guards, the knights, and the prisoners—but not the hounds.

The knight drew back his sword as Si Kon held up his hands. "My Prince, why have You forsaken us?" he cried out.

The hounds immediately ran over to attack, and the Vincero Knight allowed it, reveling in the vicious onslaught.

Dalton could hardly move as he witnessed the sacrifice his friend had made. "Please let him live, my Prince," he whispered, and quickly made his way to the swords.

Now all attention was on Si Kon and the attacking hounds. Other knights quickly came to the scene. Painfully aware of the screams of Si Kon, Dalton removed the top sword, being careful not to make a sound. Once it was in his hand, he realized it was his own, for he had been the last prisoner to arrive in this dreadful place.

"Release!" He heard the Vincero Knight call out.

There was only a moment left, and Dalton was too far from the nearest cell. He moved quickly toward it, but he was still twenty paces away.

"You two get him to his cell, and the rest of you get back to work," the knight commanded.

Dalton considered returning the sword, but now even that was too late. There simply was not enough time, and he would soon be the next meal for the hounds of despair.

He glanced at Si Kon and then toward the cell. To his astonishment, another prisoner stood at the opening with his hand outstretched. Dalton quickly threw the sword the last fifteen paces, hoping the man would catch it. The sword turned end over end once. Then the prisoner caught the hilt with one hand and the base of the sword with the other, cradling it to his bosom. He disappeared into the cell just as the hounds returned to their post near the swords. They sniffed all around the pile of strewn swords as if something was amiss but finally settled to their former guard positions.

Dalton held his breath another moment until he was certain no one had seen his theft. He quickly made his way to Si Kon and took the place of one of the prisoners carrying him. His brave friend was a bloody mess, and Dalton's heart broke at the sight of him. One of the dogs had reached his face, and another had torn into his thigh. Once in Si Kon's cell, Dalton quickly set to cleaning and bandaging the wounds as best as he could.

"Si Kon, you gave too much," Dalton began, but Si Kon grabbed his tunic and pulled him close.

"When I came, Drox said he would destroy my two daughters if I ever tried to escape. If you make it out…tell them I live!"

Dalton swallowed hard. "I will, my friend. I promise."

TEN

FLEEING THE DARK

Waiting for his sword took every ounce of Dalton's self-control. He wanted to just walk down to Lim's cell and get it himself, but that would double his exposure time outside his cell. And so he waited. He stayed close to the iron bars near Si Kon's cell and dared not speak. He listened for the slightest noise. Hearing nothing left him both relieved and impatient.

Dalton's left arm was still very weak. He had wrapped it tightly to his torso to keep the upper bone from twisting. He could use his hand and a bit of his lower arm but that was all. He hoped the dressing wouldn't hinder him too much if he were faced with a fight. The tie to the wrap was at the front, so all he had to do was pull the knot open with his right hand, and both arms would be available in case of an emergency.

Dalton wasn't sure how much time had passed, but it felt like hours. At various times throughout the sleep period, a guard would walk the perimeter of the outer chamber near the prison cells. Dalton lay still as he heard the guard's footsteps approach and then fade away to his left. Shortly thereafter, he heard Si Kon slowly sliding across the floor, but it was too dark in the cells to see if he was carrying the sword.

"It is here," Si Kon whispered and held the hilt toward Dalton. As Dalton grasped the sword, Si Kon grabbed his forearm.

"Be careful, my friend," Si Kon said soberly. "Drox doesn't give second chances."

"Thank you, Si Kon. I'll not forget you."

Dalton stood and tucked the hilt of the sword under his left armpit, holding the blade along the left side of his body with his right hand. He crossed over to the cell entrance and peered into the outer chamber. The snores coming from various cells interrupted the cavern's otherwise heavy silence. He quietly exited his cell to the left and stayed close to the iron bars of the next thirty cells, hiding behind rock outcroppings whenever possible. He tried to synchronize his steps with the rhythm of the loudest snoring man.

When he reached the last cell, he heard the footsteps of another guard making rounds. He was amazed that so much time had already passed and began to worry that he would not make it out of the cavern before the waking alarm.

Dalton froze, wondering where he should hide. The footsteps came closer, and he heard the man in the cell behind him moan. Dalton quickly entered the cell and crouched in the far corner near the man's boots, hoping the guard would be sloppy in his inspection. Evidently the bundle beneath his blanket in his own cell had fooled the guard, for he had already passed by it without alarm, but now Dalton was sure to be captured.

The torch the guard was carrying flickered with his gait and caused the shadows of the bars to dance in a passing parade. Dalton sank into the rock walls like a cornered mouse. He clutched his sword and decided he would at least fight to the very end. He heard his fellow prisoner stir on the far side of the cell just as the guard reached it.

Dalton held his breath.

"Hey! Do you mind?" Dalton heard the prisoner say loudly, holding up a hand against the light. The guard looked briefly to the far side of the cell and then away as he passed. The light diminished, but Dalton saw the prisoner slide the waste bucket away from him. After a moment of silence, the man crept near to Dalton.

"Whether you make it or not, you bring us hope," the man whispered in the murky darkness.

Dalton sighed and moved to the cell opening. He waited until the silence swallowed the receding footsteps of the guard and then made his way to the cavern opening. He felt a cool breeze flowing downward, and it refreshed his spirit to know this air came from a place with no ceiling. Dalton looked about once more to verify he was yet unseen, grasped the hilt of his sword with his right hand, and entered a wide tunnel that sloped gently upward.

The tunnel curved left and right, then divided. The right branch was dark and unlit. It appeared to be a dead end, so Dalton took the left branch, which was illumined with an occasional torch. There was still no sign of Drox or his henchmen, and Dalton became anxious over what he might find at the tunnel's exit.

After a few more moments of travel in near darkness, the subtle glow of natural light began to illumine his way. He could hardly contain his excitement as he neared the exit. He forced himself to slow his pace and proceed with caution, fearing the exit might be guarded.

To his surprise and delight, there was no one. He looked into the beauty of a pink and blue morning sky. The smell of evergreen and wildflowers filled his nostrils. He plotted the quickest route to cover, then bolted away from the tunnel opening toward two pine trees with large lower branches that sagged nearly to the ground. He dove beneath the trees, wincing at the pain the motion brought his arm. He looked behind him for pursuers, but there were none. His heart was racing wildly.

Dalton tried to calm himself and regain his nerves as he considered his next move. He plotted another path farther away from the tunnel opening and moved quickly and quietly to put as much distance as possible between himself and Lord Drox's henchmen. With each step he took, he dared to wonder if he had truly succeeded.

After a few more minutes, Dalton's thoughts turned toward getting his bearing within the region where he found himself. The terrain was a strange mix of trees, brush, grass, sand, and rock. He crawled to the top of a rocky knoll to gain a better vantage point and peered over the top of a boulder, looking back toward the tunnel entrance.

He discovered that the tunnel was a natural formation in the side of a tall granite wall. As he followed the wall with his eyes, he grew dismayed. The wall continued in both directions and joined again behind him some two hundred paces away, forming a box canyon with no apparent escape.

He searched the canyon walls for a place he could scale, but they were nearly vertical, a treacherous climb for someone with *two* good arms. Besides this, he realized that even if he could climb the walls, he would be in the open for a long time—easy prey for Drox and the Vinceros.

There must be another way out of the canyon, he thought. He decided his only course of action was to follow the canyon walls until he found the way out. With the tunnel entrance to his right, Dalton began to carefully navigate his way along the base of the canyon wall. As he went, he came across the bones of what must have been a prior prisoner. Four inverted horseshoe-shaped stakes held the wrists and feet of the skeletal victim, whose bones the death ravens had presumably picked clean. Dalton knelt down near the skull. He was so appalled and disturbed that he found it difficult to continue.

How does one become so evil to be able to do such a thing? he wondered. Righteous anger kindled within him, and he moved onward. As he went, he discovered more heinous sites of execution, and fear began to creep into his mind, robbing him of his courage.

Had these unfortunate victims tried the very thing he was now attempting? Was his demise inevitable?

By midafternoon, Dalton had made it three-fourths of the way around the canyon and was nearing the tunnel again. He was thirsty, hungry, tired, and frustrated by his lack of success.

How close to the tunnel dare I go? he asked himself. *Surely they have discovered my absence by now. Why aren't they searching for me yet?*

Dalton could not quell the apprehension that rose within him. His search was becoming desperate. He looked ahead and still saw no indication of an opening in the walls of the box canyon.

His next move required him to travel across an open area with very little cover, but he had no choice if he was to continue. He looked toward the tunnel opening, then slowly walked across the rocky floor of the canyon, ready to drop low at any moment.

Then he heard it. A low, wicked chortle flowed across the rocky floor and enveloped him like the wispy, dark ghosts of an evil apparition.

Dalton turned, then froze. He dared not close his eyes, but he wanted to. He thought that perhaps if he closed them long enough he would awaken from this nightmare.

But the nightmare had just begun…

ELEVEN

RETURN TO TIME

Dalton awoke from his dream of memories and into the reality of a nightmare. The burning pain of Drox's blade in his abdomen screamed in his mind as well.

"My Prince, help me!" he cried out as tears fell from the corners of his eyes and ran down his temples...tears of pain, tears of humility, tears of sorrow.

Dozens of huge double-winged ravens landed near him, and he knew it was only a matter of time before the agony of their tearing beaks increased the pain of his pierced torso tenfold. He grasped the grisly blade once again and lifted with all his might, but the pain made his attempt paltry. He covered his eyes with his hands to protect them and felt the ravens descend on him like a thick black thundercloud. But the world of unconsciousness mercifully swallowed him before any flesh was torn from his body.

♛ ♛ ♛

The way of a fool is right in his eyes,
But he that listens to counsel is wise!

The lyrical words of this strange song were faint and hollow to Dalton, but as his mind lifted from the fog, the voice became clearer.

A lying tongue is a brief endeavor,
But the lip of truth will last forever!

The voice seemed to belong to an aged man. He hummed the tune when there were no words to sing.

Dalton tried to open his eyes, but every fiber of his body, including his eyelids, felt as if they were crushed by the granite of a mountain.

"Am I dead?" he asked.

He heard the shuffle of old feet coming toward him. He opened his eyes enough to see a blurry figure bent over him.

"Yes, you are," the old man said. "Well…not quite."

Dalton tried to lift his head but as his neck muscles pulled taut, his abdomen shot barbs of reminder pain to stop him. He winced.

"Where am I?"

"Well, you're not in the bellies of twenty death ravens, and you're not wrapped around a blade of steel." The old man lifted his chin slightly and peered down his nose at Dalton as if to get a closer look at him. "You are in my cave, and I don't really like visitors, so you'd best be on your way now."

Dalton was extremely confused, and the babblings of this old fellow weren't helping.

"Off you go now…off with you."

Dalton tried to roll to his side and moaned in deep pain.

"Not well enough?" The old man looked concerned. "I guess you can stay awhile longer, but you'll have to compensate me when it's time."

"Who are you, sir?" Dalton asked as he looked closer at the strange character.

"I'm a collector."

Dalton squinted in his confusion.

"I take old things and make them new," the old man said with a grin. His full head of white hair flowed to the back of his neck. His eyes were deep blue and did not look wild or deranged. The gentle wrinkles on his face seemed to have been formed by joyful smiles rather than by scowls or burdensome toiling. His welcoming countenance contradicted his dismissive words.

"For example…," the man continued. He shuffled to a table nearby where he had tools and polishing instruments. It took considerable effort, for he was slightly bent and walked with a hindered gait. "Here are two buckles that I found cast aside. One is old and tarnished, but look at this one."

Dalton turned his head with effort. The bronze buckle gleamed in gnarled, wrinkled hands.

"See how beautiful it is. Both of these looked like the first, but with the right tools and some hard work, this one shines brilliantly."

Dalton didn't care at all about polished buckles. He turned back and closed his eyes. The longer he was awake, the more miserable he felt. He wondered if his death had just been postponed a day or two.

"I'm thirsty," he said, realizing he hadn't drunk any water all day.

"You should be… It's been days since you've been here. You've taken a few sips of water, but that is all."

The old man brought a cup to Dalton and helped him lift his head to drink. The water was cool and refreshing. It tasted sweet, and when Dalton finished the cup, he asked for more. It seemed to wash him from the inside out.

Dalton suddenly realized that his enemy might be near. Surely it would be impossible for this old man to drag him very far.

"Lord Drox—where is he?" he asked with eyes wide.

"Lord Drox?" the old man tilted his head.

"Yes, the one who pierced me through. The mighty warrior who has imprisoned many knights."

"Ah...you speak of the one named Skia Ek Distazo." The old man nodded. "He is the one you fear."

"The one everyone fears."

The old man smiled. "Not everyone."

Dalton took a breath. "You do not know him then."

"True, I do not know him—only of him."

"Is he near?" Dalton insisted.

"I have not seen him here," the man said, and poured another cup of water from a jar. "Distazo has no use for an old man like me."

Dalton realized there was truth in that statement. Perhaps Drox wouldn't think to look in the cave of this old man, at least for a while. He looked at the old man and realized he was probably in grave danger and didn't even know it.

"Thank you, kind sir. I am eternally grateful to you."

The old man stopped and looked into Dalton's eyes. He smiled gently and put a hand to Dalton's chest. "Rest, young knight."

Dalton took a deep breath and felt peace sweep over him. He closed his eyes.

"What is your name, good sir?" he asked.

"I am Mister Sejus. What is your name?"

"I am Dalton of Salisburg, and I'm..." Dalton found it impossible to form the last of his words, and he was pulled once more to sleep. He heard Mister Sejus begin humming again, the unsung words echoing in Dalton's dreams...

The way of a fool is right in his eyes,
But he that listens to counsel is wise!
A lying tongue is a brief endeavor,
But the lip of truth will last forever!
Forever...forever...forever...

TWELVE

THE MYSTERIOUS MISTER SEJUS

Dalton opened his eyes and took a deep breath. It took a few moments for him to remember where he was. Then he looked around and realized Mister Sejus was absent. The cave looked as though the old man had lived there for many, many years. Dalton was lying on the only cot, and it appeared that Mister Sejus had been sleeping on some blankets not far away. Dalton spotted two oil lamps that were probably used during dusk and early morning, but the cave entrance was wide, allowing slanted rays of daylight to illumine the interior. Was it late evening? Early morning? Dalton couldn't tell.

Just inside the entrance was a three-footed bronze cooking pot with a variety of pots, pans, and clay jars nearby. A fire burned beneath the cooking pot, and the exquisite aroma of the contents made Dalton's stomach howl in hunger. Near the cooking area stood a small table with two stools. A long workbench nestled along the far side of the cave wall with an organized array of tools along the back. On the right side of the bench, spread on a cloth, lay an assortment of brightly polished cups, buckles, and trinkets, while a sizable pile of rusted and tarnished hardware lay on the dirt floor to the left. Near the foot of Dalton's cot, a cushioned chair with a lamp and small stand created a cozy vignette. A similar stand hugged the head of his cot.

Dalton heard the faint sound of Mister Sejus's humming and singing. The sound grew louder as the man himself appeared in the cave entrance.

"Ah, the sleeping Sir Dalton awakes!" Mister Sejus smiled as he unshouldered a shabby pack and laid it on the table. "I can imagine you are quite hungry by now."

"I am, sir." Dalton carefully lifted his head. He waited for the intense pain of his abdomen to return, but it did not. He was relieved, though puzzled. Surely it should take longer to heal from such a grievous injury.

He looked down. The lower portion of his torso was wrapped tightly with white cloth. Then he shrugged. *Perhaps I shall live after all,* he thought.

Mister Sejus lifted the top of the cooking pot and used a polished ladle to fill a bowl with fragrant soup. He set it on a stand and helped prop Dalton up by placing a pillow and another blanket behind his head and shoulders. This movement did revive some of the pain he'd felt earlier, but with far less intensity. Dalton tried his best to move slowly and carefully.

Mister Sejus then sat on a stool beside the cot and lifted a spoonful of soup to Dalton's mouth. Dalton sipped and swallowed. He thought he had never tasted anything so delicious in all his life. He looked at the old man in amazement.

"This is wonderful!" he exclaimed.

Mister Sejus smiled. "It contains an herb that will help heal your body as well."

Dalton finished the bowl and asked for another. "I am indebted to you for your kindness," he said as Mister Sejus moved to refill the bowl. "I'm certain this has been quite an inconvenience for you."

"Yes, well I've grown accustomed to your presence, and I suppose you are still too weak to leave, so what's an old man to do?"

You are an odd fellow, Dalton thought as he watched Mister Sejus return with the soup. He lifted several spoonfuls to Dalton's mouth.

"Where in the kingdom are we?" Dalton asked between swallows.

Mister Sejus paused with spoon in the air and squinted at Dalton. "Are you planning to come back with thieves and steal my treasures?"

"Of course not." Dalton nearly laughed as he thought of Mister Sejus's "treasures" but caught himself. "I was taken captive by Lord Drox, and I have no idea how far from home I am."

This seemed to satisfy Mister Sejus. "Ah," he said and continued with the soup—but still didn't answer his question.

"How long have I been here?" Dalton asked.

Mister Sejus paused again, closed one eye, and looked to the cave's ceiling, seeming to ponder the question.

"Nine days," he finally said. "Your wound was particularly difficult to heal." He shook his head. "It is fortunate I was nearby to hear you call out, for you wouldn't have survived long with those nasty death ravens about you."

"But how did you…" Dalton tried to imagine this old man shooing away two dozen ravens, pulling Drox's sword out of the ground—and out of him—and hauling his body out of the box canyon back to his cave.

"Yes?" Mister Sejus brought another spoonful of soup to Dalton's lips.

"How did you save me?"

Mister Sejus leaned forward and stared into Dalton's eyes, startling him with the intensity of his gaze. "I may be old, young knight," he said, "but I am not weak."

It wasn't what he said, but how he said it. Suddenly Dalton became aware of something strange in the old man's demeanor—something that made the hairs on his neck stand straight. He swallowed hard and resolved to be on his way as quickly as possible.

"How far—," Dalton began again, but Mister Sejus held up his hand to silence him.

"Your questions are misguided, young one. It is your life that has intruded upon mine, so I will ask the questions now." Mister Sejus set the spoon in the bowl. "Tell me, Dalton, what is important to you?"

Dalton was taken aback at the personal question, which seemed completely beside the point.

"Excuse my asking, sir, but why do you want to know?"

Mister Sejus gave an annoyed sniff. "Because if I am going to make you well, I want to know that my time is not being spent on foolishness."

Dalton didn't answer at first. Clearly there was more to this hermit than first appeared. Besides, no one had ever asked him a question like that, and he was not fully prepared to answer it.

"There is a fair maiden," Dalton finally said and smiled as he thought of Lady Brynn. "I hope to one day win her heart and her father's approval."

Mister Sejus slowly nodded. "Kingdoms have risen and fallen on the quest for such a love. Where did you meet this fair maiden?"

"At the haven in Salisburg."

"Haven?" Mister Sejus asked.

"Yes, our place of training for the Knights of the Prince," Dalton replied.

"You serve the Prince?" Mister Sejus asked with wide eyes.

Dalton was surprised that word of the Prince had made it to the ears of this old hermit.

"Yes, how have you heard of Him?"

"When one has lived as long as I, one hears of many things." Mister Sejus set the empty bowl on the bedside stand and crossed over to the table. He picked up his pack and began lugging it slowly back toward the cot. "If you serve the Prince I know of, then you must be a mighty knight indeed."

Dalton's countenance fell. He did not feel mighty at all, especially now. He wasn't sure he had *ever* felt mighty as a Knight of the Prince. He rested his head back against his pillow.

"No, Mister Sejus. I am not so mighty a knight."

"But I am told that such knights carry the passion and the power of the Prince in their hearts. How can it be that you don't? Knights of this order claim that the Prince is the mightiest of all."

The old man's questions were beginning to burn in Dalton's soul. He wished Mister Sejus would mind his own business.

"Evidently I am not as mighty!" he retorted.

"Evidently." Mister Sejus let his pack fall to the floor and sat down on the stool again. He reached into the pack and pulled out the pieces of Dalton's sword.

"You collected my sword?"

"Of course. I told you—I collect things, even broken things...like you." Mister Sejus smiled, but it didn't make Dalton feel any better.

"This is the mark of the Prince." Mister Sejus looked closely at the hilt of Dalton's sword and nodded. "You must be telling the truth."

Dalton rolled his eyes in annoyance and shifted stiffly against his pillow. Unfortunately he was a prisoner to the old man's bantering. Mister Sejus held the sword's blade with his left hand and the hilt with his right. He fit the two pieces together and looked closely at the fracture.

"Strange," he mumbled.

"What?" Dalton asked.

"I know these swords well. A sword of the Prince is also a sword of the King. They are not supposed to break!"

"Yes, well, as you can see, mine did."

"There is only one reason why a sword of the King would break, and that is if the one who holds it does so without skill."

Dalton had had enough. Who was this old man to criticize his skills as a knight? He tried to straighten, indignation warring with pain

"I have trained and served on many missions for the Prince. There isn't a knight in the kingdom who could stand against Drox and survive. What do you know about battle anyway, old man?"

Mister Sejus slowly put the two pieces of Dalton's sword on the stand nearby. He pursed his lips together as he looked at Dalton's bandaged midriff, then into his eyes.

"You have the sword and the mind of a Knight of the Prince, yet you lack."

Dalton closed his eyes and shook his head as he sagged back into his pillow.

"What gives you the right to say such things?" He looked at Mister Sejus again. "You say I lack. But exactly what is it that I lack, old man?"

The old man put a finger to Dalton's chest. "You lack the heart. Serving the Prince takes all three."

The words were so blunt they left Dalton speechless. Tears welled up in his eyes as he realized the truth of the message. Never before had his soul been laid so bare. He felt pierced again, but this time in his heart and with a different sword.

Mister Sejus creaked to his feet.

"You are weary, young Dalton. Lie down and rest again." He removed the blanket from behind Dalton's shoulders, then crossed over to light the nearby lamp. "I find that the morning always refreshes the body, soul, and spirit."

So it was evening. Dalton had not even realized that the entrance to the cave was darkening.

He closed his eyes and did not think that he could sleep just yet, but he did.

THIRTEEN

A PLACE OF BEGINNINGS

When Dalton awoke, it was morning. He heard Mister Sejus working at his bench across the cave, still humming his silly song. He lay still, thinking about their conversation the day before. He had never been so angered and enlightened by a single conversation.

Other than being famished, Dalton felt much better than he had since coming to this place. Even his left arm felt nearly whole again. He brought his right leg over the edge of the cot and set his foot on the floor. He leaned carefully on his right elbow and slowly pushed to a sitting position. At first he felt lightheaded and nearly had to lie down again, but that feeling slowly dissipated. He put his hand to his bandaged midsection and was amazed to find it only slightly tender.

Mister Sejus turned on his tall stool and looked at Dalton. "Feeling well enough to sit now?" He smiled and crossed over to Dalton. "Well, there's progress. Soon you'll be walking about, and I will have my home back."

Dalton managed a weak smile. "I want to apologize for my anger yesterday. I've been thinking about what you said."

As Mister Sejus walked toward him, Dalton noticed that he seemed less encumbered in his walk this morning. *Perhaps his joints are affected by the weather.* Dalton had heard other old people say that. Mister Sejus sat down on the stool next to the cot.

"I'm not sure how you knew, but you were right." Dalton put his hand to his head. "But how do I get a heart for something I already want?"

"Now you are asking the right questions, young knight." Mister Sejus smiled and stood. "But first it is time for you to eat."

He supported Dalton and helped him stand, then guided him to the table.

Mister Sejus fed Dalton a sumptuous breakfast of eggs, sweet corn muffins, stewed pork, and fresh fruit. He encouraged him to drink much water as he ate. Dalton finally wiped his mouth, feeling energized by the meal.

"Come, Dalton," Mister Sejus stood at the cave entrance.

Dalton stood carefully, with a hand across his stomach, and joined the old man at the entrance of the cave. Dalton squinted at the brightness of the day, for the sky was full of blue and sun.

The hermit's cave was elevated enough to offer a spectacular view for a great expanse in all directions. Off to the right, a majestic mountain range stretched far into the distance. In front of them, the land dropped away to forest and then gave way to a lush green plain, with a river that wound its way out of view. The terrain to the left was more rugged but just as enchanting.

"What do you see?" Mister Sejus asked as he gazed into the distance.

Dalton was now leery of answering the man's questions too quickly. When he hesitated, the old man looked at him with inquisitive eyes.

"An accident or a plan?" Mister Sejus continued.

"You are a strange fellow, Mister Sejus. Where do you come from?"

The old man smiled again and seemed a little disappointed. But he answered the question. "Nowhere...and everywhere. My business of collecting takes me to many places in the kingdom." He turned again to look at the morning scenery.

Dalton gazed at the man, amazed. At first he had thought him a crazy hermit, then a meddling old man, but now…

"How are you feeling?" Mister Sejus said without looking at him.

Dalton put his hand to his stomach again. "Quite well, actually." He was surprised to realize how true that was. "I think I should be on my way within a day or two."

Mister Sejus just nodded. "Very well. In the meantime, you can earn your keep by helping me."

He brought Dalton to his bench and set a stool next to him. Dalton sat down as the old man went to his huge pile of rusted trinkets. He scrounged around a bit and finally pulled something from beneath the pile.

"Ah, here it is. I knew it was in there somewhere."

Mister Sejus held a crusty old sword that looked like it had been weathered in the elements for a hundred years. He placed it on the table before Dalton.

"You must polish this for me. If you do a fair job, perhaps it will help me recover my costs for treating you."

Dalton looked at the sword with dismay. The double-edged blade was dull, with streaks of rust down its length. The handle and guard were so dirty and tarnished that Dalton could not make out the markings. Cleaning the weapon looked like a hopeless task. But he knew he was indebted to the old man, so he determined to do his best.

The hermit taught Dalton how to work the polishing tools, and he settled into the task, starting with the blade. When he tired, he rested on the cot for a bit before returning to the chore, pushing himself to concentrate on his seemingly impossible assignment. He was glad, though, when Mister Sejus called him to the table and afterward suggested an early night.

Over the next few days, Dalton's strength returned. As they worked at the bench together, Mister Sejus found many opportunities to ask more probing questions which Dalton found uncomfortable to answer. There was something about the man that drew Dalton to him, and yet he wanted to be done with the nagging questions about purpose, vision, and knighthood. He had never worked so hard to answer questions before. In fact, all of Sir Dornan's training seemed simple and trivial compared to this.

Dalton wasn't much more thrilled about his task of cleaning the sword. The work was tedious, and the old hermit would take nothing but perfection.

"You must polish in the direction of the grain of the steel," he said to Dalton during one of his inspections. "The blade was forged and folded in that fashion and must be worked according to the designs of its swordsmith."

At the end of the fourth day, Dalton had completed only one side of the blade, but his feelings about the work were beginning to change. He was amazed at the beauty that was slowly being revealed by his labor and by the guidance of Mister Sejus. Part of him almost wished he would be there to finish the task, but he was feeling much better and anxious to be on his way.

The next morning, he stood just inside the cave with the knapsack full of provisions Mister Sejus had given him. "I want to thank you for all you have done," he said to his elderly host, "perhaps even risking your life to save me. I'm sorry I didn't finish the sword for you, but it is time for me to be on my way back home. My family will be worried."

Mister Sejus nodded and held Dalton's gaze for some time…until Dalton turned to look out the entrance.

"Your family…and your Lady Brynn." Mister Sejus stated, as if he knew Dalton's thoughts.

"Yes, but I still don't know where I am and which direction to travel."

"That is a truth for certain," Mister Sejus said. "Are you sure you're ready to leave?"

Dalton looked back at the hermit, a bit exasperated. "I am ready."

Mister Sejus slowly nodded. "I see. And what of Lord Drox? Are you ready for him?"

Dalton hadn't thought of that evil warrior for many days. Once again, this old hermit had slapped him in the face with the simple truth of the obvious. Dalton felt a rush of fear rise up in him. Drox was surely nearby.

"If you leave now, he will find you and imprison you or kill you."

The old man spoke the words so poignantly that Dalton stumbled in his heart.

"Why do you think he sought you out and pierced you through?" Mister Sejus added.

Dalton was quiet. "Because I lack," Dalton said softly. "When I was first taken prisoner by Drox, a friend and fellow knight searched for me." He thought back to that stormy night. "This mighty warrior hid from my friend as though he were afraid of him."

"What was different between you and your friend?" Mister Sejus asked.

Dalton looked away, into the kingdom. "Koen rides as a knight with authority…as though he *knows* it is all true."

"Ah…he *knows* it is true."

Dalton turned to look at the hermit again. "Is it that simple?"

"The only way to have a complete heart for the Prince is to *know* it is true. A man who doesn't is like a wave of the sea being tossed by the wind. Eventually, Drox will find that man and imprison him…or pierce him through."

"So what do I do?" Dalton voiced the question but not necessarily directed toward the old man. He didn't expect him to be able to give him an answer.

Mister Sejus looked warmly at Dalton. "Travel with me today, young knight, and I will show you the answer to one of your questions."

"*One* of my questions?" Dalton asked.

"Yes…one of many that keep you from having the heart of a Knight of the Prince. You must face all of them, Dalton. The King and His Son are not afraid of questions."

Mister Sejus went into the cave and retrieved his own pack, already prepared. He lifted it to his shoulder.

"I thought you wanted to be rid of me," Dalton said with a smile.

"Yes, well, I'm afraid you're just not ready, and I must be patient. What's an old man to do?"

At first, Dalton wondered if the pace of the hermit would be too slow for him to bear, but he quickly discovered this was not the case. It was Dalton who struggled to keep pace with Mister Sejus. Dalton himself needed frequent rests, for his strength was still greatly diminished. They traveled east along the base of the mountain range for most of the morning.

"Now I recognize these mountains," Dalton said with satisfaction. "These are the Northern Mountains. I was so close to them that I could not see them for what they are."

"'Tis often true in life, young one," the old hermit said without skipping a step.

At one point, they climbed a ridge. Mister Sejus stopped for a moment, and Dalton was grateful. The old man seemed tireless. They looked south to a thick forest.

"This is Wolf Ridge," Mister Sejus said and pointed to an area not far away. "There was a great battle there long ago."

"Here in the Northern Mountains?" Dalton asked between ragged breaths. "I've not heard of it."

"You wouldn't have, but the kingdom hung in the balance. The people are often unaware," Mister Sejus said. "There are many who don't even believe there is a King."

"Yes, I know," Dalton said. "Those are the ones most difficult to tell about the Prince."

Mister Sejus shook his head. "Without a King, there is no kingdom. The King established Arrethtrae long ago. Those who live here and deny His existence live a life of contradiction, for the kingdom itself testifies to His reign."

By early afternoon, they came to an area that seemed forgotten by time itself. It was a scene of ancient beauty, and Mister Sejus slowed to enjoy it. A sparkling river flowed nearby, tumbling gently over shallow waterfalls. Mister Sejus told Dalton it was the Tisgri. The trees seemed larger than usual and widely spaced, and the ground between them was padded with thick grass and soft mats of forest moss. Green vines and brightly colored flowers provided a garden atmosphere, and a delightful canopy of leaves and pine branches filtered the sunlight into golden spires. Dalton looked around in awe at the magnificence of it all.

They walked quietly through the trees until they came to the ruins of a forgotten estate. The outer walls had crumbled, and the rusted iron gates had fallen from their hinges. They walked through the gate and stood in the outer court of what once must have been a majestic palace.

"What is this place?" Dalton asked in wonderment.

Mister Sejus breathed deeply. "This is the place of beginnings... This is Nedehaven."

They stood before the blackened ruins of a great and ancient palace. The trees and vines had nearly swallowed the structure, and it looked as though it was trying to return to nature, but its residual magnificence was unmistakable.

"I thought this story was just a fabricated legend," Dalton said, still gawking at the ruins. "I never would have believed such a place existed."

Mister Sejus turned to Dalton. "That is why we are here."

Dalton looked at the old man, who seemed to have become stronger by their day's hike rather than weaker. The young knight followed him up the overgrown stairway to the veranda of the great hall. Dalton brushed the dirt away from a broken piece of marble that had fallen from its place above the entrance. He traced his finger in the engraving: Nedehaven.

"This truly was it," he whispered.

Dalton followed Mister Sejus through the ruins to a back courtyard, where the remnants of a stone walkway wound its way through an abandoned garden. Mister Sejus stopped and knelt down. He placed his hand on the stones, now nearly overgrown with moss.

Dalton knelt beside him.

"The King walked with Peyton and Dinan here," Mister Sejus said quietly.

Dalton looked once more at the ruins and realized that this truly was the place of beginnings—the place where the King first established his perfect kingdom under the rule of Sir Peyton and Lady Dinan. He looked at the charred remains of the palace and imagined it burning as Lucius and his Shadow Warriors brought the terror of their battle to Arrethtrae. He was kneeling in the heart of the kingdom...and of the King himself.

"I doubted that such a place existed." Dalton hung his head, ashamed. "It seemed too far-fetched to be truth, and yet..."

Mister Sejus turned his head and looked at Dalton. "The Prince came to Arrethtrae because of the failure here long ago. Through Peyton's failure, all people of Arrethtrae were doomed. Without the resounding truth of this place, this story, there is no foundation for the truth of the Prince, or even the King, for that matter."

Mister Sejus looked deep into Dalton's eyes. "If you don't believe in the beginning, you can't believe in the Prince or in his mission to rescue the people of Arrethtrae from the clutches of the Dark Knight."

Dalton was crushed by the force of the man's words.

"I'm such a fool. Why did I doubt so?" Dalton said, fighting back his emotions.

"It is such with so many," Mister Sejus said sadly as he looked at the ruins of the palace. His sadness seemed to come from deep within his heart.

Dalton put a hand on the old man's shoulder. What had unnerved him about the man before now sparked a desire to know more.

"How do you know such things, Mister Sejus?" he asked, slowly shaking his head. "How?"

Mister Sejus looked at Dalton again. "Come back with me and work on my sword, and I shall tell you more."

Dalton nodded. He thought about how his perception of this old hermit had changed over the past week, and with it his perception of the kingdom...of everything.

FOURTEEN

DIVIDING THE CODE

The journey to Nedehaven had proved a strain for Dalton, and he needed a few days to regain his strength. But Mister Sejus was true to his charge and helped Dalton fully recover. Dalton was now feeling nearly whole again. When Mister Sejus removed the bandage one evening, Dalton was shocked to see that there was hardly a scar to show for the steely invasion just three weeks earlier.

"It seems impossible!" Dalton exclaimed as he felt his stomach and his back at the same time.

Mister Sejus peered closely at the wound site. "Your healing is not yet complete, so you must not strain too much."

Dalton nodded as he donned his torn and bloodstained tunic. "You are a remarkable old man."

Mister Sejus ignored the comment. "Let's see how your sword is coming."

The blade was now completely polished, and it reflected the light of the nearby lamp with a spectacular sheen. The edges still needed work, and the guard and handle were clean but not polished yet. Still, Dalton was pleased, and so was Mister Sejus.

Dalton picked up the sword and moved into a hanging guard stance. It felt good in his hand. The balance was perfect.

"Set your feet here and here," the hermit said as he tapped the floor with his toe. "And you must turn your wrist a bit more."

Dalton furrowed his brow and opened his mouth to shoot out a barbed comment. After all, he had been trained at the haven in Salisburg and in the advanced training class at Brimwick Downs. Who was this old man to tell him anything about sword fighting? Then he realized that whenever he said such a thing in the presence of this peculiar man, he usually ended up embarrassed and humbled. So he shut his mouth, listened, and obeyed.

Over the next two hours, Mister Sejus instructed Dalton on the fine points of swordsman's stances. Slowly Dalton's mind opened to the fact that this old hermit was well versed in the techniques of advanced sword fighting.

When they stopped, Dalton lowered his sword and stared at Mister Sejus. He was certain this was not the same man who had nursed him back from the dead, for the man seemed twice his former self in mind, stature, and strength.

"Once again you have surprised me, Mister Sejus," Dalton said as he laid the sword back on the workbench. "You have shown me forms that not even my instructors knew. How much more do you know?"

Mister Sejus lifted the sword and wiped it with a rag as he inspected the handle. "When you have finished polishing the handle, I can show you one or two more things," he said with a quick grin. "Tell me, young Dalton, what directs the thoughts and actions of a Knight of the Prince such as yourself?"

"I suppose it is the training we receive from our instructors."

"I see," Mister Sejus said as he returned the sword to the workbench. "And what if an instructor is incompetent or misdirected himself? What then happens to his students?"

Dalton had no answer.

"Would it be safe to assume that his students might become incompetent or misdirected?"

"I suppose so," Dalton replied, once again uncomfortable.

"Men are flawed, Dalton. What has the King given us to guard against such a thing?" Mister Sejus asked. "What *should* direct the thoughts and actions of a Knight of the Prince?"

Dalton knew this answer from his training. "The Code and the life of the Prince."

Mister Sejus penetrated Dalton's soul with his eyes once again. "Your words are true, but do you *believe* them, Dalton?"

Dalton wanted to say yes just to stop this dialogue, but this confounded hermit seemed to read his heart like an open book. He would take nothing short of a truthful answer.

"I was taught that the Code is an archaic document that our kingdom has outgrown—a relic from the past that is only a rough guide." Dalton bent over, put his elbows on the workbench, and rested his fingers on the sword. "Some even said that it was not given by the King but written by the hands of mere men. Deep inside I know it is more than that, but most of the kingdom has rejected it—including many men of great learning." Dalton turned his head and looked at his peculiar mentor. "So how does one truly know what to believe or follow?"

Mister Sejus looked on Dalton as a father would, patiently teaching a son through his years of experience.

"The Code is timeless, Dalton. It was not given to one man in secret for a particular time, but to all people openly for all time. It is not a parchment in the inner chambers of the palace of Chessington, but a living creed written on the fleshly tablets of the hearts of men and women who serve and love the King. The Prince is the personification of the Code. By Him the kingdom lives or dies. Do not let the vain teachings of wayward instructors cause you to wander from the resilient truth of the Code and the Prince! Test it, Dalton, and see if it is not true."

Dalton looked at Mister Sejus and knew he spoke the truth. Why had it taken him so long to see it? This is what his friend Koen believed, and it was the reason he was a knight of authority.

At the haven in Salisburg, Koen and Carliss had stood firm by the Code in spite of ridicule. Dalton had not. Now he turned away and knelt to the floor on one knee, crushed by the weight of his past compromise. He lowered his head.

"I hardly know the Code," he said softly. "How can I live by it?"

Dalton felt the gentle hand of Mister Sejus on his shoulder.

"Honor the King with your life. Swear allegiance to Him and to Him only," the confident voice of his mentor spoke over him. Dalton lifted his eyes and joined his voice with Mister Sejus's in quoting the Code he had learned by heart when he first became a knight.

"Serve the King in truth, justice, and honor. Offer compassion to the weak, the destitute, the widowed, and the poor. Live for the King, and serve others without cause for personal gain. Never abandon a fellow knight in battle or in peril. Equip, train, and prepare for battle against the forces of the Dark Knight. Serve the King and faint not in the day of battle. Use not the sword to seek selfish gain, but rather to execute justice and the will of the King. Be merciful, loyal, courageous, faithful, and noble, but above all, be ye humble before the King and before men. Let your words be always spoken in truth."

Dalton stood and turned to look at Mister Sejus. "I understand—and believe. As with Nedehaven, I now see how it is impossible to fully serve the King without the Code."

"Yes," Mister Sejus nodded.

"You have taught me so much." Dalton gazed at the man as if he had just wiped the fog from a window and seen him anew. "Teach me more...*Master* Sejus."

FIFTEEN

SIR DALTON, KNIGHT OF THE PRINCE

Dalton put aside his misconceptions of Master Sejus and freed his mind to accept the powerful teachings of his new mentor. Per Master Sejus's instruction, Dalton meticulously polished the handle of the sword and discovered the ornate and intricate mark of the King in its pommel.

Master Sejus made a final inspection of the beautiful weapon. "Still some work to do on the edges, but it is a magnificent piece."

"I had no idea that such a superbly crafted sword was beneath the rust and tarnish," Dalton said.

"Even the treasures of a king are oft neglected, but it does not diminish their value." Master Sejus handed the sword to Dalton. "It is yours now."

"But my labor is my payment to you for your help and kindness," Dalton protested.

"Help and kindness are not such if they are purchased," Master Sejus said as he went to the pile of rubble at the back of his cave.

"Besides, how could one's labor ever repay the saving of a life? Therefore they are a gift—both your life and the sword."

"Thank you. I shall wield it with skill and not let it break as before."

Just then Master Sejus pulled another old sword from the rubble and held it before him. "Let us make sure of that," he said with a smile. "Follow me."

Dalton followed Master Sejus out of the cave and into a shallow green valley not far away. They faced each other with swords ready. Dalton guarded his mind against the notion that Master Sejus would be an easy spar.

"Remember what I taught you about your stances, and we shall proceed from there."

After just two quick engagements, Dalton quickly came to understand that Master Sejus's words of instruction were girded up by a complete mastery of his sword. Their swords clanged in the arena of the valley, and Dalton became a student of a true master. By day's end, Dalton hardly dared to speak, for today had revealed the silliness of his prior thoughts and words.

As they walked back to the cave, Dalton followed behind and stared at the strong shoulders of his master. He wondered how he could have ever thought this man was feeble and old. There were moments in their training earlier that Dalton saw glimpses of superiority he had never seen in the hands and movements of any other swordsman.

Dalton spent the rest of the evening in quiet contemplation. That night he lay down on the blankets on the cave floor, silently offering the cot back to his mentor.

When morning came, Dalton rose up solemn, with eyes downcast.

"What is on your mind, young knight?" Master Sejus asked as they ate breakfast.

Dalton briefly looked at Master Sejus and then down to his tin plate.

"I am sorry, Master Sejus. I have played the fool and did not know how great a man you were." He lifted his gaze to the penetrating blue eyes of his mentor. "Please forgive me."

Master Sejus leaned across the table and placed a hand on Dalton's forearm. "You saw me as you believed I was. It is not I who have changed, but you. Now set your eyes on the King and His Son, and live the Code!"

"I will. I so swear!"

Over the next three weeks, Master Sejus taught Dalton, and he was transformed into a superb swordsman and a bold knight. Each morning Dalton woke in anticipation and fell to sleep exhausted and amazed. As the strength of his body returned and increased, so did the strength of his heart as a Knight of the Prince. His respect and adoration for Master Sejus became something he could not express in words. He came to expect the unexpected from his teacher.

One morning in the valley, Master Sejus gathered a bundle of sticks and stood five paces away from Dalton.

"You have learned many important techniques for mastering the sword, Dalton, but you must learn to respond quickly to the advances of your adversary. Speed is life." Master Sejus selected one stick from the pile at his feet. "Ready yourself."

Dalton was confused until he saw the master throw the stick toward him. He swiped at it with his sword and missed. The stick struck his forehead with a thud. He rubbed his head with his left hand and looked quizzically at his teacher, but Master Sejus simply grabbed another stick and prepared to throw again. After three more attempts, Dalton became frustrated.

"Focus not on the stick, but on one small part of the stick. See small and aim small; then you will hit the stick." Master Sejus reached for another one.

The stick flew toward him. He missed again, but this time his eyes captured the image of a single knot on the side of the stick as it came tumbling toward him. It was as if his mind was able to freeze the moment in time as the stick hung suspended in air.

"I saw the knot," Dalton said, amazed that he was able to focus on such a minute detail during its motion.

"Good, now strike the knot."

Another stick came. Dalton froze the moment and struck with his blade. It hit, and the stick was immediately deflected to his left.

Soon Dalton was successful nearly every time. As he progressed, Master Sejus threw the sticks faster. Dalton's earlier frustration transformed into enlightenment as his speed and focus as a swordsman reached an entirely new level of expertise. Two days later, he had mastered the drill.

"Now you must learn to apply this to divergent enemies. You will not always face a single warrior, but often two or three will attack at the same time. It is the way of evil."

Master Sejus instructed Dalton to pretend to fight an invisible warrior as the sticks were thrown. It was difficult at first, but soon Dalton was able to momentarily divert his attention to hit the sticks with hardly a break in his advance or retreat.

That evening, Master Sejus prepared some of the same delicious soup that Dalton had eaten when he first awoke in the cave weeks earlier.

"Dalton, I have shown you Nedehaven and the origins of the kingdom," Master Sejus said, ignoring his own bowl of soup. "I have helped you see the evidence of the King in everything that surrounds us. You have come to fully believe in the Code, and you now understand the great love the King has for the people of His kingdom. I have also trained you in the art of the sword, and you have mastered it."

"I am grateful beyond measure, master," Dalton said as he set his spoon aside, sensing the importance of his mentor's words.

Master Sejus paused. "All of what I have taught you is for naught if you do not understand the cornerstone of it all."

"Cornerstone?" Dalton asked.

Master Sejus took a deep breath.

"What do most people say about the Prince?" he asked.

Dalton thought about all the comments he had heard throughout his travels with other knights as they tried to proclaim the Prince. He even remembered the conversation with the boy back at Salisburg. Dalton closed his eyes as he realized that those words had influenced and confused him at times.

"There are some who say that the Prince is not truly the King's Son."

"Who do they say that He was?"

Dalton opened his eyes. "Some say He was simply a great teacher… and a master of the sword, but that is all. Others say He was a raving lunatic."

"Consider those statements about the Prince, Dalton, and know that He was neither. If He was simply a great teacher He would not have made such preposterous claims about being the King's Son. And a raving lunatic will rarely have followers who are willing to lay down their lives for him. Furthermore, I have never found a lunatic to be a true master of the sword. No, young Dalton, the Prince was neither just a great teacher nor a lunatic. He was exactly who He said He was: the King's only Son. And because of the King's great love for His people, He sent His Son to Arrethtrae to live, teach, and die for them. Anyone in the kingdom who believes anything less than this is not one of His knights and will not enter into the Kingdom Across the Great Sea."

Dalton considered Master Sejus's words and felt the foundation of his knighthood settle upon the rock of truth. From this day forward, he knew he would never be moved from this place. It was as if the bright and shining sun had hardened the flimsy clay of his mind into a wall of commitment to the King and to His Son. Master Sejus had boldly asked

Dalton to challenge the core of his service to the Prince and then showed him the way. The doubts that had plagued him for years were wiped away.

He looked at Master Sejus and once again stood in awe at the depth, and width, and height of the wisdom of this man. He was more noble than any knight, lord, or duke he had ever seen, and yet he lived in this cave. How could such a thing be?

He nodded. "I understand, master. The Prince is the cornerstone of it all, and I am fully committed to Him."

Master Sejus stared into Dalton's eyes. "I believe you, for I see it in your eyes. You no longer have to be afraid of anything or anyone."

The following morning, Dalton awoke to see Master Sejus packing his knapsack.

"Where are we off to today, master?" Dalton asked, wiping the sleep from his eyes.

Master Sejus paused and looked at him. "Prepare yourself, young knight."

Dalton quickly rose and ate. The stool upon which his clothes lay now also held his chain mail. His armor also lay nearby. He hadn't worn it since the day Drox's blade had pierced him through. Both the chain mail and the armor had been repaired.

He looked at Master Sejus. A sadness swept through him as he watched his master finish packing. Dalton quickly dressed but hesitated with the chain mail and armor.

"It is time, Dalton. You are ready," Master Sejus said.

Dalton hung his head. His heart became heavy as he realized that this would be his final day with Master Sejus. No one had made such a dramatic impact on his life as this man had. He wondered if his newfound confidence would flee from him once out of the presence of this master swordsman.

Dalton donned his chain mail and armor, and they left the cave together. They passed through the training valley and onto a ridge, where it seemed to Dalton that the horizon stretched on forever. He looked far to the south, where he now knew his home lay. As his thoughts turned to Lady Brynn, he felt the strong hand of Master Sejus on his shoulder.

Dalton turned and realized he was looking up into the fiery eyes of a virile, noble knight. *How could this possibly be the same feeble old man of six weeks ago?* he wondered.

"Dalton, do you see that small village just there?"

"Yes."

"That is Lewerton. Find the stables and speak to a man named Yergillay. Tell him Sejus has sent you."

Dalton was perplexed.

"He will arrange for your travel back home," Master Sejus said.

Dalton turned his eyes from the horizon and back to Master Sejus. "You saved my life...in more ways than one. Drox's prison is full of men and women just like me. I want to help them."

Master Sejus was still staring at the horizon as he slowly nodded. "Yes. Drox's prison is a daunting one. He imprisons only the Knights of the Prince. And its strongest bars are not of iron." He turned to look at Dalton. "Drox's prisoners are not all like you, Dalton."

"Why do you say that, master?"

"Because you fought to leave that place and most do not. You were seeking the truth and lost your way in the wilderness. Many lose their way in the wilderness seeking to avoid the truth. Such are some of them."

Dalton stood there many minutes, pondering what his mentor had said. "I have so much more to learn from you, master. I don't want to leave you."

Master Sejus smiled. "The skills I have taught you, Dalton, will stay in here forever," he said as he put a finger to Dalton's temple. "But *I* will be in *here* forever," he said and placed his hand on Dalton's heart, "just as *you* will be in *here* forever," and placed his other hand on his own heart. "Besides, there is a young lady out there who needs you."

Dalton could not resist the urge to kneel before him, though he didn't fully understand why. There was something beyond noble about Master Sejus, and only as Dalton's wisdom and skill increased had he been able to see it.

"You are so much more than a collector!" Dalton said.

"Yes, but that is my most important role. You see, Dalton, I collect broken and tarnished treasures and make them priceless!"

Dalton saw himself in those words, and his eyes welled up with tears. "I will never know how or why you came to me when I was dying in Drox's canyon, but I thank you. I owe you my life, Master Sejus."

Master Sejus smiled and gripped Dalton's shoulder.

"Rise up, Sir Dalton, Knight of the Prince. Rise up and be strong!"

Dalton stood, and the two men embraced. Master Sejus grasped Dalton's shoulders and looked deeply into his eyes.

"Drox will come for you, and you must face him alone."

Dalton lowered his eyes but Master Sejus squeezed his shoulders tighter.

"You are able. Remember who you serve."

Dalton lifted his eyes and felt the power of the Prince renew his strength.

"The King reigns," Master Sejus said.

"And His Son!" Dalton exclaimed with authority he had never spoken nor felt before.

Master Sejus smiled and nodded. He turned to travel west, and Dalton set his eyes to the south. Master Sejus walked a few paces but turned to face Dalton once again.

"Dalton, I came to you because you called for me."

He then turned again, walked down the ridge, and disappeared into the trees.

"I called for you?" Dalton whispered to himself, puzzled, as he thought back to that dreadful day.

SIXTEEN

BACK FROM THE DEAD

Dalton's walk to Lewerton took most of the morning. It was just as Master Sejus had said. Yergillay gave Dalton a courser, a horse trained for travel and war, to make his trip to Salisburg. Dalton promised to treat the animal well and return him in a few days' time.

By midmorning of the third day, Dalton arrived home. His father and mother wept with joy, for they had thought him dead. They talked at length, and Dalton shared his incredible story with them over the delicious meal his mother hastened to prepare. Dalton learned that his parents had asked Koen to quarter Chaser for a time. He would need to ride out tomorrow to collect the horse—but today he was much more concerned about another reunion. As soon as he felt he could leave his parents, he hurried to see Lady Brynn.

Dalton rode up to the manor, and a servant took his horse. He was escorted into the parlor and waited for Lady Brynn to come. Another servant disappeared up the staircase, and moments later he saw Brynn rush to the top of the rail, looking down in disbelief.

"Dalton?" she whispered.

Her eyes opened wide as she realized that it truly was him. She ran down the staircase and fell into him as he wrapped his arms around her.

"I can't believe it's you," she said through her tears.

"I've returned and have so much to tell you."

Brynn stepped back and wiped her tears. She laughed, then cried more, then became angry. "Why did you wait so long to return?"

Dalton grabbed her hand and led her to a bench nearby. They sat, and Dalton told his bizarre story. It was strange for them both, for Dalton had never spoken so passionately about the Prince. The words felt and sounded strange to him, which he did not expect. Lady Brynn squirmed at times, not from his portrayal of the hounds of despair or the death ravens or even his near fatal wound, but from the fervor of his newfound devotion to the Prince. He realized this was new for her, and he tried to soften his words a little, allowing her space to adjust.

When he finished, she looked up at him and smiled—a little indulgently, he thought. She lifted a hand to his cheek. "I'm just so glad you're back. Please don't ever leave me again."

Dalton smiled but could not respond, for his thoughts were already preoccupied with devising a way to set his fellow knights free from the bondage of Drox.

"I'm glad to be back too," he finally said.

They enjoyed many hours together, and Dalton was amazed at how often he spoke of the Prince. For some strange reason he didn't yet understand, it brought tension to their relationship. Brynn always seemed eager to change the subject, and she talked a lot about her plans to travel and see the rest of the country.

The following day, Dalton traveled to Koen's farm to greet his friend and retrieve his horse. He went first to the stables and found Chaser. He tied up the borrowed courser and then rode Chaser to the front of Koen's home.

Lacy was the first to see him, and she ran into the house shouting as he dismounted. Koen's entire family rushed into the front yard. Koen ran to him first, with eyes wide, and hugged him like a lost brother. Dalton was surprised, for this reunion seemed warmer and more enthusiastic by far than his time with his parents or even Brynn. He hugged Koen back and looked at Carliss over Koen's shoulder. She was smiling bigger than he had ever seen before.

Dalton released Koen and hugged each of the members of the family in turn. Carliss was last. She put her arms around his neck and squeezed him tightly, then quickly released and turned shyly away. Dalton had to suppress a smile as he turned his attention to little Lacy, who had slipped her hand into his.

Koen's family invited him into their home, and they sat around the kitchen table as he told his story. The entire family hung on each word. They were a silent and motionless audience that eagerly soaked up the tale. Here, his passionate words for the Prince brought smiles and nods. It was so different yet natural, and he felt at home. When he finished, there was a unified sigh of relief. Not a word of his story was questioned, and they showed deep concern for the rest of Drox's prisoners.

Koen's father put a hand on Dalton's shoulder. "You've inspired us, Dalton. I would love to one day meet this Master Sejus."

"I hope to return and meet with him again. I have so much more to learn," he replied.

"What will you do now?" Koen asked.

Dalton looked at each of the faces that were staring at him. "I'll have no peace as long as I know that a place like Drox's prison holds fellow knights in bondage. I will go back."

The family looked solemnly at him.

"You can't go alone," Carliss said.

"You're right. He is too powerful for one man, and the Vinceros and guards there are many." He looked at Koen and his family. "Will you come with me to petition the haven for help?"

Koen reached out and grabbed his arm. "We are all with you."

Dalton felt like he was amidst brothers and sisters. "Thank you," he said with relief.

When it was time for Dalton to leave, he went to get the horse Yergillay had loaned him, but it was gone. Koen's family helped him search the nearby countryside, but there was no sight of the horse. Dalton despaired, for the borrowed horse was a fine animal and it would take him a long time to earn enough to pay Yergillay back.

"It is strange," Koen's father said. "We've never had anything like this happen here before. I'm sorry, Dalton."

"It's my own fault," Dalton replied. "I must have tied him too loosely." His joyous reunion was sobered by the animal's disappearance, but there were larger concerns for the time being.

The next morning, accompanied by Koen, Carliss, and their father, Dalton rode back into Salisburg, but his appearance before the subcouncil of knights and other prominent members of the haven at Salisburg proved to be a disappointment. They gave his tale only a lukewarm reception, and he felt he had to convince them of the truth of it.

"You say there are no locked doors on the cells?" one knight asked. "I find it quite…incomprehensible that the prisoners would just stay there. Why don't they leave?"

"Fear keeps them there. Fear that Drox will hunt them down again," Dalton replied.

"Why haven't we seen evidence of this before?" another knight asked.

"I don't know," Dalton said, exasperated. "Perhaps you are not looking!"

Sir Treffen stood. "Dalton, it isn't that we don't believe you. We just need more to go on before we act. Where is this prison you speak of?"

"I don't know," he replied, realizing that he had never asked Master Sejus of its whereabouts. At the time, he hadn't considered attacking it, for he was preoccupied first with healing and then with being prepared if Drox ever came back for him.

One of the knights rolled his eyes and turned aside.

"But I know someone who can find it," Dalton blurted out.

The council conferred quietly for a moment; then Sir Treffen spoke. "We will send two knights to accompany you to find the location of the prison. When you have discovered it, report back, and we will then decide what to do."

"I will go with him," Koen stood up from the back of the room.

"And I," Carliss joined her brother.

Dalton turned and looked at his friends—true friends.

"Very well. So let it be. This meeting is adjourned," Sir Treffen announced.

Dalton took a deep breath, and Koen, Carliss, and their father came to him. Koen's father looked disappointed.

"It is not enough," he said shaking his head.

"What should we do?" Dalton asked.

"Do as they say, but be careful, and do not allow yourselves to be discovered. Meanwhile I will send for Sir Orland." Koen's father thought for a moment. "Dalton, show me your best guess on a map as to the location of Drox's prison, and describe some of the landmarks if there are any. We must be ready to strike quickly."

Dalton nodded. "We will first ride to visit Master Sejus. He will show us the way to the prison."

They decided to take one full day to prepare and leave the following morning.

How in the kingdom will I tell Brynn? Dalton wondered.

Dalton, Koen, and Carliss set out for the Northern Mountains the following day. They traveled north along the Frates River to Kaar Lake and then northwest to the foothills of the mountains. They arrived in Lewerton late in the evening and spent the night there. The next morning, Dalton went to the stables to explain what had happened to the horse

Yergillay had loaned him and to promise repayment, but the owner of the stables knew nothing of the man or the horse.

"But I was here a week ago," Dalton insisted, scratching his head.

"You didn't talk to me," the barrel-chested man scoffed.

"No, I didn't. Yergillay met me in the evening and brought the horse to me." Dalton looked about, searching for the stableman that gave him the horse.

"Which stall was the horse in?" the owner asked.

"The far one on the end," Dalton pointed. He looked briefly at Koen and Carliss, wondering if they were beginning to think him mad. "It was a fine horse…a courser."

"Look," the owner said angrily. "That stall hasn't held a horse in over a month, and I have never heard of this man you call Yergillay. Be gone from me. I don't have time for such nonsense when there's work to do."

Dalton squinted and shook his head. *What is going on?* he wondered. *How will I find Yergillay and repay him now?*

Lewerton was small, and it didn't take Dalton long to confirm that no one in the village had ever heard of a man named Yergillay. Puzzled, they left Lewerton and headed up into the mountains.

They rode in silence for a while, for Dalton was preoccupied with the strange disappearance of the animal no one had seen and the man he had borrowed it from. After a few miles, Koen teased Dalton about it briefly, then engaged him on talk about their mission. Dalton's spirits gradually lifted, and by late morning, as they neared Master Sejus's cave, Dalton could hardly contain his enthusiasm. He cantered Chaser up to the cave and dismounted.

"Come!" he exclaimed, encouraging Koen and Carliss to join him.

They climbed up the gentle embankment that led to the cave and entered. Dalton gawked in stunned silence, for the cave was completely empty—void of any evidence that anyone had ever been there.

Dalton ran his hands through his sandy hair, his eyes open wide. "He was here, I tell you!"

Koen and Carliss briefly glanced toward each other.

Dalton frantically searched for any shred of evidence to validate his story but found none. There was not even a footprint in the dirt.

"This is where the cot was…and here was where we cooked…and over here was a chair." Dalton walked rapidly from place to place, imagining each item. "Here…here was Sejus's workbench with all the tools and trinkets." He spread his hands out as if he could feel the bench beneath him.

He turned and looked at his friends in confusion. "What's going on, Koen?" he asked.

Koen put a hand on his shoulder. "I don't know, my friend. You've been through a lot these past few months."

Dalton looked at his friend and hated to think that he too wouldn't believe him. "You do believe me… Don't you?"

Koen hesitated only an instant. "Yes, Dalton. We believe you."

He looked toward Carliss for support, and she nodded. "Let's find Drox's prison."

"All right," Dalton sighed. "All right."

As they left the cave, Dalton hesitated at its opening and looked back.

Am I mad? he wondered for a moment, then shook himself and exited.

"Do you have any idea where to look for the prison?" Koen asked.

Dalton looked out into the country, and it seemed as though they were trying to find a needle in a haystack. The land seemed so vast.

"It must be less than a day's journey from here, for I can't imagine Sejus being able to carry or drag me much farther," Dalton said as he considered the possibilities. "He had no horse. The Frates River is to the east, which would be difficult to cross, and the Northern Mountains are at our backs to the north. I came home via the southern route and saw no sign of it. So it must lie somewhere to the southwest." Dalton swept his hand across a fairly rugged region of country.

Although he tried not to show it, Dalton was discouraged. What if they never found the canyon? Would anyone—even his best friend—ever believe him? What of the prisoners? Were they doomed to a death of abandonment? What of Si Kon, the brave soul who helped him escape? Dalton closed his eyes and relived the terror of those weeks in his mind to convince himself his ordeal had indeed been real.

"Are you ready, Dalton?" Carliss asked. She sat tall on her horse, Rindy.

Dalton opened his eyes and looked at her. He searched her eyes, seeking...he didn't know what. Hope, perhaps.

She smiled and raised an eyebrow. Dalton nodded.

"Let's go," he said and slapped the reins of Chaser.

Dalton, Koen, and Carliss searched the countryside for four days, sweeping across the terrain in search of the box canyon. Each day they traveled, the possibilities expanded and their chances of success seemed to shrink. After three days more, their supplies were nearly exhausted and they were farther from the cave than one person could ever have carried or transported a near-dead man.

On the morning of the eighth day, they rose up to begin their travel back to Salisburg, and Dalton fell into silent despair. Even Koen seemed a bit morose.

"We will resupply and come back to search again," Carliss said, trying to encourage Dalton. She mounted Rindy.

"It's no use," Dalton said as he finished packing his horse. Discouragement pulled at his every movement. "We could search for months and not find it. It's a hole in the ground. We could be right next to it and not even know it." Dalton prepared to mount his horse. "What a fool I've been," he said.

Carliss shook her head. "No, you're not a—"

"Draw your sword." Without warning, Koen had appeared at Dalton's side, weapon ready.

Dalton stared at him, bewildered.

"What are you doing?" Carliss asked her brother.

"Draw...your...sword!" Koen took a stance.

Dalton slowly drew his sword. Before he had it completely out of the scabbard, Koen attacked. Dalton instinctively finished his draw and thwarted the slice. Koen thrust again and did not hold back. Dalton defended each cut and slice, and as he did, he felt the power of the Prince rise up within him.

The impromptu duel escalated to a voracious volley of swords. Dalton felt the mastery of his blade and took the offensive against Koen. Faster and faster his blade flew until Koen was in steady retreat. In one blazingly quick maneuver, Dalton crosscut and thrust at Koen's heart with the speed of a panther. Carliss screamed, and Dalton pulled back on his blade at the last moment, stopping the tip of his sword at Koen's chest.

Both men were breathing hard. Koen held up his arms, acknowledging his defeat. He then pushed Dalton's blade aside and sheathed his sword. He walked up to Dalton and stared into his eyes, just inches from his face.

"Three months ago I could have easily defeated you," Koen said between breaths. "Today you are a master. No imagination or fabricated story could do that."

Dalton closed his eyes, thankful for the wisdom of his friend.

Koen put his hand on Dalton's shoulder. "You have been with the Prince, my friend, and no one will ever take that from you."

Dalton opened his eyes wide as he considered Koen's statement. Deep in his soul he had known that Master Sejus was someone much greater than a mere Arrethtraen, but he had never suspected that he might truly be in the Prince's presence.

The hairs on the back of his neck stood straight. He trembled both from excitement and respectful fear as he realized it was true. All that time he had been with the Son of the King.

Koen sheathed his sword and went to his horse. "We will search again until we find this dreadful place."

Dalton nodded and walked toward Chaser. He looked at Koen and Carliss as he swung into the saddle, grateful for that day they came to the haven—even more grateful for the day they had become his friends. "Any ideas where we should—"

Caw! The familiar, terrifying sound made him jerk his head to the left. Far in the distance, a lone raven circled high in the sky.

"There!" he exclaimed. "There is where the canyon is!"

Koen and Carliss looked at the distant bird and then at Dalton.

"Are you sure?" Koen asked.

Dalton kept his eye on the raven. "As sure as I have been with the Prince!" he exclaimed. "Follow me."

Dalton was once more filled with the confidence of the Prince. He kicked Chaser into a full gallop toward the circling black speck in the sky…but now there were two.

Seventeen

DEATH RAVENS

Dalton, Koen, and Carliss tied their horses a safe distance from the edge of the canyon and carefully made their way through the trees. As they neared the canyon walls, they crawled the last twenty paces on hands and knees. Dalton peered over the edge with Koen on his left and Carliss on his right.

"Is this it?" Koen asked.

Dalton scanned the floor of the canyon more than ninety feet below them, trying to orient what he had experienced down there with his new perspective up here.

"It looks like the same canyon, but I can't be sure. Wait...yes...I recognize that outcropping. You can just see the cave entrance beside that grove of trees over there." Dalton pointed down to their left.

"Look!" Carliss whispered as she pointed through a break in the trees to their right.

"I don't see anything." Dalton squinted and looked to where she pointed.

"Nor do I," said Koen.

"Just to the right of those trees—on the ground!" Carliss's tone indicated urgency.

Dalton leaned close to Carliss to line his sight up with her finger and followed the line down to the canyon floor. His stomach rose up in his throat as former fearful memories and emotions flushed through him.

"No!" Dalton whispered.

Koen backed away and came up on Carliss's right side to get a better view. A fellow knight was staked to the ground. Dalton looked up and saw two dozen death ravens circling high above them.

"I'm going down!" Dalton exclaimed, unable to peel his eyes from the man on the ground.

Carliss and Koen stared at him.

"That is not the plan, Dalton," Koen said firmly. "The three of us can't take on this stronghold by ourselves. You said there were at least a dozen guards and six Vinceros when you were imprisoned."

Dalton turned to the right and looked past Carliss to Koen.

"If we don't do something, that man will die!"

"If we go down there, we will all die!" Koen rebutted.

Koen spoke the truth and Dalton knew it, but he could not—would not—sit by and do nothing. He clenched his teeth.

"I will not let that man die like this! You two ride for help. I'm going down there."

Dalton glanced from Koen to Carliss. She was staring into his eyes. "I will help you," she whispered.

He looked back into Carliss's eyes and nodded.

Koen took a deep breath and looked back at the man. "Perhaps we can free him and get him back up here before Drox discovers us."

"I'll get the rope." Dalton crawled back a few paces, then ran to his horse. As he opened the pack, Carliss appeared beside him.

"You don't have to do this, Carliss." He quickly withdrew the rope.

Carliss unfastened her bow and quiver from her saddle and set them across her shoulder. She looked straight at Dalton.

"Yes, I do. I'm a Knight of the Prince. It's what we do."

They made their way together back to the canyon edge.

"The death ravens are circling lower," Koen said.

Dalton quickly tied one end of the rope around a tree. He scanned the rest of the canyon, then threw the rope over the edge. It caught on a ledge that jutted out halfway down.

"I will scale down first," Dalton said. "You two stay up here. If the man is too badly beaten or too weak, you will need to pull him up using the rope."

Koen grabbed his arm. "I don't like it, Dalton. I should come down with you. What if Drox or the others come for you?"

"We may need to get him up fast, Koen. This is the only way. Besides, I won't be able to keep an eye on the cave entrance down there. You'll have to watch it for me."

Dalton looked at Carliss and nodded toward her bow. "How good are you with that?"

Carliss just stared at him.

"She can shoot the eyes out of a mole at fifty paces," Koen replied for her. "While it's moving," he added.

"Good," Dalton said. "Watch the cave and watch those birds."

He checked his sword, turned his back to the canyon, and started his descent into the terrifying abode of the evil Lord Drox.

Dalton made it to the ledge where the rope was caught. He gathered the remaining rope with one hand and threw it out and over the ledge, then took a moment to look up at Koen and Carliss. Koen was pointing to the man on the floor, and Carliss was reaching for an arrow.

Dalton felt his heart pound, knowing he was exposed to the whole canyon here, and he wondered if someone was coming. He knew he would have to hurry.

Just then he heard the man below him yell. Dalton looked over the edge of his perch and realized that it was not someone, but something that had concerned Koen and Carliss. The death ravens were now only a few feet above the man, spiraling down on their final descent.

Whoosh! Carliss's arrow flew straight toward the staked man, and Dalton wondered if the poor soul would die by her arrow rather than by the death ravens. The man screamed as the first three birds landed right beside him.

Thud! The arrow landed just on the far side of the man, right next to one of the ravens. The half-dozen ravens bolted into the air in a frenzy.

Dalton decided to quicken his descent, for he knew that Carliss would not be able to hold off the ravens for long. He had positioned himself and made a step downward when he heard a slight whistle from above.

He looked up to see Koen's eyes wide in angst. He pointed, and Dalton followed the line until his eyes came to rest on the death ravens. They were no longer circling above the staked knight but flying straight for Dalton.

It took him a moment to comprehend what was happening. *Could these ravens be that aggressive?* he wondered. It was almost as if they were guardians of the canyon, like bees guarding a beehive.

Dalton shook himself from the sight of two-dozen death ravens getting closer to him by the moment. He gripped the rope and continued his descent as quickly as possible, but he had made it only a few feet before the first raven swooped in on him.

Caw! The bird screeched while it dove straight for Dalton's head. He pulled in tight to the canyon wall and just missed being pecked by the enormous black beak. The double wings of the bird gave it incredible maneuverability, and it turned in an instant for another attack. This time it came closer and sank its beak into Dalton's back. The pain nearly caused him to lose his grip.

The bird dropped down and back to gain speed and make way for the next attacker. Dalton took the momentary break to take two more steps down, then prepared for the next bird as it closed in. Just as it began its dive, Dalton heard the *swoosh* of another arrow.

Caw-aw! The bird screeched as Carliss's arrow pierced its right double wing. It fluttered end over end downward, ending up impaled against the rocky landing below. Dalton breathed a sigh of relief and quickly descended four more lengths. Another arrow *whooshed,* and another raven fell lifelessly to the ground.

The other ravens seemed to hesitate, and Dalton made the most of the pause in their attack. He looked up and realized that with a few more feet of descent, the ledge would put him out of sight of Koen and Carliss and therefore out of their protection from the death ravens. He looked down—nearly thirty feet to go.

The ravens seemed to rally, and two of them dove once more on Dalton. Several more ravens flew toward Koen and Carliss, while three others landed on the ledge that the rope was drawn tight against—a divergent attack that left Dalton amazed. How intelligent were these birds? Koen and Carliss were now occupied with their own protection, and the three ravens on the ledge set immediately to pecking at the rope.

Dalton tried to descend farther, but one raven tore a piece of skin off the back of his leg, where no chain mail protected him. Another was coming in on his back again. At the last moment, he pushed away from the cliff edge and loosened his grip on the rope, hoping that he could control his descent. The rope screamed through his leather gauntlets, and he squeezed to slow himself.

The death ravens swooped again but missed. Dalton's speed increased beyond what he could control, and he wondered if he would survive the fall.

Just before impact, he gripped the rope with all his might, and it slammed him against the side of the canyon wall. He felt the rope sever above him, and he fell backward the last few feet, crashing onto the jagged rocks below. Half of the rope tumbled down on top of him from the ledge up above.

He rolled out into the open, in view of Koen and Carliss once again, and the ravens swooped down on him. Carliss found a split second to aim and launch another arrow toward the nearest bird. Pierced through one of its wings, it fell to the ground near Dalton, flapping its other three wings wildly in protest.

Dalton was on his back, trying to recover, and the wounded bird came at his face. Dalton held out his hand to protect himself and the bird latched on to it with a viselike beak. Dalton grabbed its neck with his free hand and wrenched it away, hurling it onto a rock beside him. He jumped to his feet, drew his sword, and dived under the nearest tree.

Those blasted ravens. Now how will I get out of here? he wondered.

After a moment of fruitless pursuit, Dalton's remaining ravens left him and joined in the attack on Koen and Carliss. He watched his comrades retreat out of sight into the trees behind them, and he paused a second to plot his course. Then he ran and knelt beside the man who was a fellow knight.

"Who are you?" the man asked with wide eyes full of fear.

Dalton didn't answer. Instead, he sheathed his sword and set to lifting the U-shaped stakes from off the man's wrists. They were set deep into the ground, and he struggled to lift them even a little.

"I am Sir Dalton," he said as he strained. "I was once a prisoner here. We haven't much time." He finally managed to lift the wrist stakes enough for the man to free his hands, but the stakes at his feet seemed nearly immovable. The man tried to help, but with his legs pinned down, there was little he could do. Being so exposed unnerved Dalton, and with every second he imagined a blade piercing him through from behind. He pulled up with all his might and was able to free one foot.

"Hurry!" the man said in near panic just as Dalton lifted the last stake from his foot...but it was too late.

EIGHTEEN

THE SWORD AND ITS KNIGHT

"Once a prisoner, always a prisoner!" A deep, dark voice echoed off the canyon walls and filled Dalton's heart with dread.

Dalton turned on his knee to see Drox coming toward them. The knight next to Dalton cowered like a beaten puppy. "No...no...no," he moaned.

Dalton fought the urge to join in his abhorrent fear as the ominous form of Drox loomed larger with each step.

"I must say that you have surprised me, knave," Drox taunted as he drew his grisly weapon. "I have never had an escaped prisoner of mine actually come back to my stronghold on his own. You must be a fool of fools," he bellowed in laughter.

Dalton's mind flashed to his previous encounters with Drox, and he remembered the absolute power of his sword. This felt the same. Rattled by a powerful sense of déjà vu, he cowered for an instant...until he remembered his time on the mountain and his calling as a Knight of the Prince.

He had been with Master Sejus.

This was not the same.

He felt a surge of strength well up inside him as never before. He rose to his feet and stood tall, his muscles quivering in anticipation of the fight to come. No longer did he doubt his purpose. No longer did he doubt the King—or the Prince! And in that knowledge of truth, he found great authority and power.

He turned and looked at the knight cowering on the ground, mesmerized by the form of Drox.

"Go tell Si Kon I'm coming," he said quietly but firmly.

The man looked at Dalton, bewildered.

"Go!" Dalton yelled.

"Yes, go knave. I will kill you later!" Drox screamed at the man as he retreated toward the prison-cave.

Dalton turned and glared at Drox. The evil lord was now within striking distance, and Dalton had yet to draw his sword.

Drox locked eyes with him, and Dalton felt the monster tremble.

"I thought I had killed you," Drox said.

"You thought wrong," Dalton answered.

Dalton slowly drew his sword, the sword he had polished with Master Sejus, and its blade gleamed brilliantly in the brightness of the sun. The reflection landed on Drox's face, and he momentarily turned away.

"I have been with the Prince," said Dalton, "and I've come to destroy you, Drox!"

"Never!" Drox screamed, and unleashed a volley of cuts and slices at Dalton.

Dalton focused on the lessons of Master Sejus and found his power in the techniques he had been taught. His sword held firm, and he felt for the subtle faults in Drox's attack. He did not retreat from the evil lord, but instead brought a steady advance against him. The crash of the swords echoed off the canyon walls in a continuous melodic rhythm of clashing steel.

At one point Drox paused and looked stunned. His eyes opened wide as Dalton assumed one of the stances that Master Sejus had taught him. It was the look of recognition—and the look of fear.

Drox raised one hand high in the air and motioned. Dalton caught movement out of the corner of his eye but dared not take his gaze from Drox.

"I don't care what you think you've learned, knave. I will kill you and feed your measly flesh to my ravens!" Somehow now the words sounded hollow, as if Drox himself only half believed them.

Drox attacked again, just as a death raven swooped from Dalton's right side. Dalton ducked from the raven and momentarily lost his concentration on Drox. This felt too familiar—and deadly. He recovered just in time to see another two-handed cut flying toward his left arm. Taking the brunt of Drox's blade would shatter his arm again, and Dalton despaired. He had fallen for the same trick, and this time there would be nothing to keep him from dying at the hands of this bloodthirsty warrior.

In the split second that remained, Dalton was tempted to jump back, hoping by some miracle to avoid the bone-crushing blow of Drox's blade. Instead, he thrust himself forward, directly into Drox's body. Drox's blade still struck Dalton, but near the hilt of his sword, with only a fraction of the original force. They both tumbled to the ground in a fray of armor and swords. The ravens fluttered wildly above them, not knowing what to strike at.

Dalton finally was able to set his foot against Drox's chest and push away. He rolled backward and onto his feet just as he saw a raven dive toward his head.

See small and aim small; then you will hit the stick. The words of Master Sejus flashed across his mind as Dalton picked one feather on the forward set of wings, just behind the head of the raven. He swung his sword in a blaze of speed and sliced the raven in two.

By now Drox was on his feet, and he stared at Dalton in shock.

Drox motioned again with his hand, but this time Dalton heightened his focus on the divergent attack and did not duck.

Drox brought a diagonal cut from the right just as a raven swooped in. Dalton met Drox's cut while simultaneously sighting a feather on the raven's underbelly. He quickly slid his blade from Drox's and swung it in a downward, then upward arc that sliced the bird from neck to tail. It hit the ground with a thud. Drox hesitated, giving Dalton a chance to cut the left wings off of the next attacking bird.

Drox and Dalton locked eyes again, but the moment was interrupted by the neigh of a horse from above. Both Drox and Dalton looked up at the canyon ridge to see a contingent of mounted knights. A glimpse of their banner brought renewed courage to Dalton. Sir Orland had arrived.

Drox stepped back, shaking his head. Another raven attacked Dalton, but he was ready. Its headless body flew into Drox's chest and splattered him with blood. Dalton felt the power of the Prince in each slice of his magnificent sword and wished for every dreadful raven in the canyon to come to him.

Drox and Dalton both stood motionless for a second. Then Drox gestured for his ravens to continue as he turned and ran headlong toward his prison.

Dalton sliced through four more death ravens until the last few disappeared over the rim of the canyon. He looked toward the retreating Shadow Warrior and found himself in a quandary. What should he do next?

He imagined Drox and his henchmen in the prison conducting countless hasty executions and realized there was no turning back now. He was too far away to give any instructions to Sir Orland, and he wouldn't know what to tell him anyway. So he pointed in the direction of the cave and ran after Drox, hoping Sir Orland would meet up with Koen and Carliss to form a plan before everyone, including himself, was dead.

He neared the cave entrance just as his enemy was about to duck out of sight.

"Drox!" he yelled, hoping to keep him out in the open, away from his reinforcements.

Drox stopped and turned.

"Is this what you truly are—a coward?"

Drox hesitated as Dalton closed the distance between them.

"You are no warrior," Dalton taunted. "You are a parasite feeding on the fears of others. You have no real power over any of the knights you hold!"

Drox could take the insults no more. He lifted his sword and took a step toward Dalton—but stopped when the sounds of fighting drifted from the tunnel behind him. He turned and ducked into the cave. Dalton reached the tunnel mouth a few steps behind him and followed him through the twisting passageway.

The sound of clashing swords grew louder as Dalton pressed onward through the corridor, his eyes gradually adjusting to the dim light. *Which prisoner has dared to draw a sword against the Vinceros?* he wondered. He could imagine only his friend Si Kon having the courage to do so, but Si Kon would not last long by himself, and neither would Dalton. Even with the strength of the Prince in him, Dalton knew that alone he was no match for Drox's force . He couldn't wait for reinforcements, though. If he delayed his aid to the imprisoned knights, they all might die. He had to reach them, to persuade them somehow to take up arms against Drox.

He had just reached a bend in the tunnel when he heard the dark voice of Drox echo through the tunnel, and the words pierced him like a dagger.

"Kill them all!"

NINETEEN

A WARRIOR'S BLADE

"Drox!" Dalton shouted as he rounded the bend and ran onward.

In the dim torchlight of the tunnel he saw the Shadow Warrior's large form pass by four figures locked in deadly sword fights at the junction of two tunnels. Dalton remembered passing the darkened tunnel branch when he exited the cave months earlier. But who—?

His eyes adjusted, and he saw the swish of long hair from one of the defenders of the darkened tunnel. Carliss! She and Koen were in the fight of their lives against two Vincero Knights.

Dalton attacked from the blind side of Carliss's opponent, and he fell to the tunnel floor instantly. Carliss took the opportunity to bring her sword against Koen's opponent. His yell for help was cut short by her blade.

"Koen! Carliss! Praise the King you are here!"

"We searched for another way in," Koen said.

"I'm afraid this is going to be..." Dalton paused.

"Let's go," Koen and Carliss said in unison, and the three knights ran into the darkness as soldiers of light.

"I saw Sir Orland and his men on the canyon ridge," Dalton said as they ran.

"They should see our horses near the back tunnel entrance," Koen replied. "They're in plain view."

"We can only hope," Dalton said. "Carliss, when we enter the prison area, be ready with your bow."

"I only have two arrows left," she replied.

"It will have to do," Dalton looked over at her as they passed by a torch on the wall. He was momentarily dazed by this spunky girl of yesteryear who had become a courageous woman of strength. What others had found so annoying years earlier at the haven, he now found captivating...her serious resolve to serve the Prince.

If only Lady Brynn..., he found himself thinking.

The light ahead outlined the huge figure of Drox standing near the entrance of the underground prison area.

"I said to kill them all," Drox was shouting. "Do it now!"

Dalton, Koen, and Carliss entered into the chaos of a bloodbath in the making. Shouts and exclamations filled the prison as a dozen guards and Vincero Knights entered the chamber. Drox's hounds of despair added their unearthly howling and vicious snarls.

Then, seconds later, the screams began.

Dalton swallowed hard, then added his voice to the commotion: "Rise up, Knights of the Prince, and fight!" He and his friends were immediately engaged by four Vincero Knights, and they maneuvered to cover each other's backs.

Dalton parried a thrust from one of his opponents and countered with a crosscut that found its mark. He saw Koen's opponent fall, and he disengaged to leave them at even odds.

"Drox!" Dalton shouted at the top of his lungs.

The mayhem subsided, and there was a peculiar pause in the havoc, broken only by the moans and cries of the wounded.

Drox turned, and Dalton hurtled toward him. "I come for you!" he shouted.

Even the Vincero Knights seemed stunned at that. No one had ever challenged the mighty Lord Drox.

Drox glared at Dalton, then glanced quickly at the odd array of spectators. He whistled and pointed to Dalton. The four hounds of despair bolted toward Dalton from various places in the chamber. Dalton stopped his advance, for it was impossible to survive the attack by four snarling dogs. Two of the hairless hounds flew past Drox and on toward Dalton, baring their fangs in anticipation of the carnage.

Swish! An arrow flew within inches of Dalton's shoulder and on toward the leading hound, but it flew wide and to the right of its target. Dalton timed a wide, powerful cut to meet the hound that was now leaping toward his throat. His sword cut through the hide of the beast. Dalton continued his slice, simultaneously turning his body to the left and ducking beneath the blur of brown hide and snapping teeth. The animal flew over the top of Dalton and landed in a motionless heap just behind him.

Dalton was now vulnerable to the second hound's attack, but another arrow *swished* passed his shoulder just as the hound was nearly to him. This time the arrow sunk deep into the animal's chest. It yelped and tumbled to rest at Dalton's feet.

The last two hounds were larger but slower. Dalton had enough time to recover for one more attack, but he could not imagine how to take two of them at once. He saw Koen attempt to come to him, but a guard impeded his progress. One hound outdistanced the other, and as Dalton prepared himself, a moment of hope filled his heart. He glimpsed his friend Si Kon lunge from a rocky ledge at the trailing hound, a dagger in his hand.

The last hound was nearly to Dalton, and he swung his blade just as before. This time the hound hesitated, and Dalton's sword cut only

through air. With his body now turned to the left, he was vulnerable, and the hound lunged for Dalton's chest.

Dalton quickly dropped his sword and drew his dagger in the split second that remained. The force of the attack pushed him backward, and he felt the powerful jaws of the beast sink into his side as he fell to the ground. His chain mail held, but the pain was severe just the same.

Dalton grabbed the dagger handle and plunged the blade deep into the side of the beast. It instantly released its bite and clamped onto Dalton's forearm. He struggled to free his arm, but the crushing jaws held firm.

Dalton dropped the knife, rolled, and grabbed the knife with his left hand as he passed over the top of it. The hound released his grip on Dalton's arm and lunged for his neck. Dalton sunk the knife once more deep into the chest of the vicious beast and this time pierced its heart. It fell lifeless on top of Dalton, and he pushed it off himself only to see a greater horror waiting.

Drox stood over Dalton with his sword pointed at his chest.

The entire chamber of the prison now fell silent as the epic conclusion of the battle between the evil master of darkness and the courageous young knight who dared return to his lair played out before them.

"Oh, how I love to kill the incompetent Knights of the Prince!" Drox's words echoed from Dalton's past. He raised his sword high in the air to strike. This time, Dalton knew Drox's target would be his heart.

"No!" Carliss's scream pierced the silence.

Dalton's courage vanished. Had his encounter with Master Sejus meant anything at all if his ending was to be the same as before?

Drox's blade began its death plunge as Dalton's mind raced through the circumstances that had brought him to this moment in time. He turned his head to the right and saw Si Kon covered in blood but standing victoriously over the brown mass of the last hound. His eyes were full of fear as he watched. This would not simply be the execution of another friend, but the final blow to his own courageous attempt to hope once more.

A glint of light shone off Dalton's blade, which lay on the ground just an arm's length away, and it told him something was different. This sword was not broken. It whispered to be used against the darkness of Drox.

Dalton once more felt the power of the Prince rise up within him as he reached to grasp the hilt of his mighty sword and brought it up to intersect the path of Drox's descending blade. There was a clash of metal, and Drox's blade was deflected to the left, where it imbedded itself in the hard ground of the chamber floor.

Drox struggled for a moment to dislodge his sword. Looking up from the ground at his nemesis, Dalton deftly set the tip of his blade just beneath the bottom edge of Drox's breastplate. He thrust upward with all his might, and there was nothing to stop the plunge of his double-edged sword.

Drox's eyes bulged in disbelief. He slowly looked down at Dalton, and his face turned ashen white. In that instant, Dalton saw three familiar faces—the mighty warrior, the young man of crafty words, and the boy of doubt years ago at the well. Three enemies who had stalked and hurt him. Three foes in one body—now stripped of power.

Dalton withdrew his sword, and Drox stumbled backward. He fell to his knees, his face contorted in anguish and rage. With one hand he clutched his chest, and with the other he raised a clenched fist into the air.

"My brothers will seek you out," he tried to scream, "and kill you all!" His weakened cry was his last. He fell face forward to the chamber floor.

Dalton stood and walked to the massive hulk of Drox's prone form. His own heavy breathing seemed to be the only sound in the midst of many hundreds of onlookers.

Dalton lifted his sword into the air. "Skia Ek Distazo...Lord Drox... is dead!" He slowly turned to see the faces of guards, Vinceros, and prisoners stunned by the moment. "By the power of the Prince, you are free!"

There was an absence of response from the prisoners, and it seemed as though the guards and Vincero Knights also didn't know what to do.

There was a clamor from the cave entrance, and all turned to see Sir Orland enter with a contingent of forty knights. At that, the Vinceros dropped their swords, and some of the prisoners began to cheer.

Si Kon stumbled over to Dalton and slowly shook his head. "You came back"—he looked once at Drox and then back to Dalton—"and defeated him. I dared not hope for such a thing."

Dalton stepped toward his friend and put a hand on his shoulder. "Together we defeated him, my friend," he said. "By the power of the Prince, we defeated him."

Si Kon's lips slowly curled into a smile. He raised his hands and yelled as Dalton had never heard before. Si Kon then fell to his knees and wept.

"I will see my family once more," he murmured through tears.

Dalton knelt down. "Yes, Si Kon."

"And I will teach my children never to doubt the Prince as I once did. Through you I have seen His might, and I will never lose faith again."

Dalton smiled and lifted his friend to his feet just as Koen and Carliss reached them. Koen grasped Dalton's arm. Carliss looked as though she wanted to hug him. She smiled instead and then quickly turned away.

"The King reigns!" Koen shouted.

"And His Son!" came the cries of hundreds in unison.

Dalton smiled at Koen. "It was your courage that inspired me," he said as Carliss turned back to him. "Both of you. Thank you!"

TWENTY

THE JOURNEY HOME

Sir Orland began giving commands to his knights, and the work of recovery and restoration began. First he gathered the guards and Vincero Knights and completely disarmed them. He offered all of them an opportunity to rejoin the cause of the Prince, but none did. Then he assigned a contingent of knights to escort Drox's henchmen to Chessington, where they would stand trial before the Council of Knights.

As soon as the guards and Vinceros were subdued, Dalton, Carliss, Koen, and Si Kon helped the other knights tend to the wounded prisoners and gather the others, explaining to all that they were free to leave. Those who had come to free the imprisoned knights were shocked when some of the prisoners refused to leave. The fear of Drox's final words still held them in invisible chains of bondage, and they could not break free. Even many of those who agreed to leave the prison seemed nearly overcome with apprehension.

"Even if we bring them out of this pit, there is only one way to truly free them," Dalton explained to Sir Orland as they discussed their options.

"What is that?" Orland asked.

"We must strengthen their hearts for the Prince and train them again," Dalton said as he recalled his weeks with Master Sejus. "I've been where they are, and only His healing power and belief in the King can overcome this."

Orland nodded. "I agree. We will take those who so desire to havens that will do what you have said. There are too many for one haven, however, so we will split them between the havens at Bremsfeld, Varlaken, and Salisburg."

Dalton, Koen, and Carliss exchanged concerned looks as they thought of the haven at Salisburg. Sir Orland seemed to understand their hesitation. "Not to worry. I've spoken to the Council of Knights at Chessington, and they are sending new leadership to the haven at Salisburg. The new trainer will arrive tomorrow. Sir Dornan has already been dismissed."

It took many hours to prepare the knights for the journey. The wounded were placed on horses and sent to Salisburg under the escort of Koen and five other knights. Dalton and Carliss remained to help with the final preparations for the others.

Carliss was adjusting the harness of her horse when Dalton found her. He tapped her shoulder, and she turned around to look at him. She seemed surprised. She wiped a few strands of hair that clung to the sweat on her cheeks and gazed at him with eyes that he now saw manifested a truly noble and courageous soul within.

"Carliss, I haven't yet thanked you."

"For what?" She loosed a brief smile, then quickly resumed her previous activity, rechecking the harness she had finished adjusting just a moment ago.

Dalton grabbed her arm, and she stopped. She looked up into his eyes.

"Thank you for saving my life…numerous times." He smiled at her. "You've quite the eye with that bow."

Dalton expected her to shy from the compliment as usual and nonchalantly resume her duties, but she did not. Instead she met his eyes with a direct gaze.

"My father taught me."

"Then I shall thank him too," Dalton said.

Carliss's eyes seemed to search his soul, and now it was Dalton who wanted to find something to occupy his hands. He realized he was still grasping her arm, and he let loose.

"I guess I'd—"

"Dalton," Carliss interrupted before he could turn away.

"Yes?"

"What will you do now?"

"What do you mean?"

"Where will you go, and what will you do?" she asked plainly.

For a moment he thought it odd that she would even care. She was such a quiet lass, and he never could tell what she was thinking.

He looked away, realizing he hadn't thought that far ahead. For the past few weeks he had been preoccupied with this very day, and now that it was gone, the future ahead seemed so open.

"I guess I will return to Salisburg and help train the knights," he said as he looked at the hundreds of knights who were preparing to leave.

"And?" she prodded.

Dalton thought of Lady Brynn. With new leadership coming to the haven, he hoped that her zeal to serve the Prince might grow. That was truly his desire.

"Lady Brynn waits for me," he said. "At least I hope she does," he added.

He looked back at Carliss. She seemed to stare through him and into the horizon behind. She nodded slowly and forced a corner of her mouth up into her signature subtle smile.

"What of you, Carliss? What will you do?"

Carliss turned back to her horse, all business once more.

"I am going with the group to Varlaken to help there."

"Varlaken... Does Koen know?" Dalton asked.

Carliss was now on the opposite side of her horse and glanced briefly across the animal's nose at Dalton. She was her elusive, serious self again.

"No, please tell him and my family for me."

"Are you sure, Carliss? I don't think Koen—"

"I'm sure." Carliss looked at Dalton with determination, and he knew she could not be swayed.

He nodded, a little confused. "I'll tell them."

The entire entourage of knights traveled east together until Carliss and one group turned southeast toward Varlaken. Half of the remainder would turn south to Bremsfeld under the command of Sir Orland, and Dalton and the other half journeyed north to Salisburg.

Something disquieted Dalton's spirit as he watched Carliss disappear over a knoll. Varlaken was not that far from Salisburg, he told himself. He and Koen would travel together in a week or so to bring her home.

He comforted himself with this as his thoughts turned to Lady Brynn and the hope of their future together.

They arrived at Salisburg on the eve of the following day, for most of the freed knights had to walk and their progress was slow. Dalton met with Koen at the haven and conveyed Carliss's message.

"Varlaken?" Koen said, concern on his face.

"Yes, she asked me to tell you," Dalton said, feeling a bit as though he had let his friend down. "I'm sorry, I should have insisted she return with me."

Koen looked at Dalton and nearly laughed. "Not much chance of that happening. Once my sister has set her mind to something, there's little chance of changing it. It's strange for her not to tell me, though." Koen thought for a moment and seemed to understand. "Working at another haven for a while will be good for her. She's been a bit sullen lately."

"Is she all right?" Dalton asked.

Koen forced a slight smile. "She will be. I'll ride to Varlaken to fetch her in two or three weeks."

"Let me know when you go," Dalton said as he mounted Chaser. "Perhaps I'll join you."

They saluted, and Dalton rode toward town. He was joyfully greeted by his family; then he ate and cleaned up. Tomorrow, before reporting for work at the haven, he planned to visit Lady Brynn. He wasn't sure what to expect, since his last visit had not been what he had hoped for. They had shared their future dreams a hundred times over the past few years, though, and living them together seemed only right…or did it?

Dalton had to acknowledge that something had changed. His recent enthusiasm for his call as a Knight of the Prince seemed to push the two of them further apart. He didn't fully understand why, but since he was the one who had changed, he felt all the more responsible for making their relationship work.

He fell asleep that night with a mind full of uncertainty. He reminded himself of one of Master Sejus's proverbs and told himself that the morning always refreshes the body, soul, and spirit. Dalton found himself humming the familiar tune, and the words of his master fell softly into his mind as he drifted off to sleep.

The way of a fool is right in his eyes,
But he that listens to counsel is wise!
A lying tongue is a brief endeavor,
But the lip of truth will last forever!

TWENTY-ONE

LOVE LOST

Dalton arrived at Lady Brynn's home in the beauty of a summer morning. She stepped outside the doorway and onto the veranda before he had come to the steps. This encouraged him, for she seemed to have anticipated his visit.

"I picked these for you," Dalton said and offered a medley of brightly colored flowers.

She gave him one of her dazzling smiles, accepted the bouquet, and leaned over to inhale the delicate fragrance. Dalton watched her and was nearly entranced with her magical movements. Her beauty radiated in the morning sunshine, and the flowers seemed dull in comparison.

So why did he feel that something was missing?

They walked to the back of her family's manor and into the garden. Hardly a word was spoken between them, and Brynn seemed content with this. Dalton finally stopped and took Brynn's hand. He turned to face her and looked deeply into her eyes. His heart began to sink as he slowly came to face the truth.

"Brynn, I came here to ask your father for your hand in marriage." He sighed. "But we both know that isn't meant to be."

Brynn's eyes saddened. She pulled her hand from his and turned away. After two steps, she turned back.

"You've changed, Dalton."

Dalton nodded. "I have."

"Why, Dalton? Why did you have to ruin…us…our future?"

Dalton stepped toward her. He took her hand in his once again. "Because it was a future void of passion for the Prince." He ached for her to understand…to change with him.

She shook her head. "You've become a fanatic. It's all you talk about, all you care about."

Dalton couldn't deny it. Serving the Prince now made the rest of life seem dull by comparison, and he was filled with this passion to serve Him. Brynn's simple statement of truth conveyed with finality the incompatible condition of each of their hearts.

In that instant, his romantic feelings for her snapped. It was a revelation that both saddened and freed him, but with each passing moment his heart lightened. He could not join to one who did not share his convictions and zeal to serve the King and the Prince wholeheartedly.

"You are right, my lady, and it is something I cannot change…nor would I ever wish to." He gently let loose of her hand and stepped back.

He looked at her once more and smiled. "I wish you all the joy and happiness you seek, Brynn."

He bowed and slowly walked away. She did not call for him, and there were no tears, only a small ache for dreams not lived.

Dalton mounted his steed and set his course for the haven. With each mile he traveled, the strings that tied him to unimportant matters of the kingdom seemed to stretch and break, falling behind in the wake of Chaser's strides. The kingdom felt big and vast, and he was thrilled to be part of something even greater than himself.

What would come next?

He was beginning to have an inkling of what he would *like* his future to hold…but he served at the will of the Prince, and he was content to let the future unfold in its own time.

♛ ♛ ♛

Back at the haven, Dalton found there was much work to be done in retraining the recovered prisoners. He offered his services to help until his next assignment was decided.

While working, he often wondered how the havens at Bremsfeld and Varlaken were doing. He was particularly curious as to how Carliss was faring. In moments of solitude, he often found himself smiling as he thought of her.

He saw Koen frequently at the haven, and they set a day to ride together and bring Carliss home. But one day well before that time, Koen failed to appear at the haven. He was absent the next day as well, so Dalton rode out to his farm to check on him.

Koen met him at the front door and stepped outside. Dalton could see by his countenance that something was wrong.

"What is it, Koen?"

Koen rubbed the back of his neck. "Father has fallen ill. Mother is quite concerned, for he runs a high fever."

"I'm sorry," Dalton said. "Is everyone else all right?"

"Yes, but I'm sure Carliss would want to know, and I can't leave mother and my younger siblings right now."

"You don't need to say another word, my friend," Dalton put a hand on Koen's shoulder. "I'm on my way."

They walked toward Chaser and heard another rider coming up the road that led to their farm. As he neared, they recognized Sir Orland. He greeted them with a smile until he realized that not all was well.

"What's wrong?" Orland asked as he dismounted.

"Father is ill."

"I'm sorry to hear that. How serious is it?" Sir Orland asked.

"I'm afraid quite. Dalton has agreed to ride to Varlaken and bring Carliss home."

Sir Orland glanced at Koen with a puzzled look. He shook his head as if he hadn't heard correctly. "Carliss?" he asked.

"Yes, she's at Varlaken," Koen said slowly as if to help jog Sir Orland's memory. "Helping with the retraining?"

Sir Orland looked as if he'd just been told an enemy was coming over the hill.

"I've just come from Varlaken. They told me Carliss left for home four days ago." Sir Orland's voice was tense. The ride from Varlaken was at the very most a two-day journey.

The three men stood in silence for a brief moment as the reality of this news sunk in. A dozen possible calamities raced through their minds. A sense of urgency swelled within Dalton.

"Are you certain?" Dalton asked.

"Sir Porvan and Lady Beda both told me," Sir Orland said.

Koen opened his mouth, but nothing was spoken. He looked back at the doorway to his home. He paced a few steps away and then returned. Dalton had never seen him so sick with concern. He looked at Dalton and Orland with eyes that pleaded for help.

"Koen, you need to be here with your mother," Dalton said as he set a foot in the stirrup. "I'll leave for Varlaken immediately."

"And I will go to the haven here and gather a search party," Sir Orland said as he too mounted.

Dalton looked down into the concerned face of his friend. "We will find her, Koen. I promise."

Dalton reared his horse and galloped at full speed toward his home, where he packed a few supplies and then set off for Varlaken. He pushed Chaser as hard as he dared, looking for any sign of Carliss along the way. His mind went wild with the possibilities of disaster, and with each episode he imagined, he pushed the horse harder.

He made the trek in record time and arrived late in the evening. He immediately met with Sir Porvan, the leader of the Varlaken haven, and

Lady Beda, a prominent knight there. Their concern was evidence that something was indeed amiss. They too were organizing a contingent of knights that would search the road and country from Varlaken to Salisburg the following morning.

Dalton talked with anyone else who had any association with Carliss. He spent a restless night and then spoke with more people at the haven. A number of the knights had seen her depart for Salisburg, but that was all. After that, she seemed to have vanished. Everyone was alarmed and concerned by her disappearance.

Dalton was frustrated by his lack of discovery. He packed his horse to join the contingent that had left earlier to search the country between Varlaken and Salisburg. Just as he was ready to leave, he heard a voice call to him.

"Sir Dalton?"

He turned about to see one of the female knights who had been rescued from Drox's prison coming toward him.

"Yes."

"My name is Raylin. I know Carliss."

Dalton looked at her and knew there was something more to come.

"Yes?" he asked.

"I didn't see her leave, and I don't have much to offer you, but I did notice that one of the other female knights left the same day. That's not so unusual, though, since a number of the knights have departed over the past week."

"Does she know Carliss?" Dalton asked.

"Yes, we all do," Raylin said. "Carliss has been so strong and helpful to all of us. Lady Salina seemed particularly drawn to her."

"Lady Salina?" Dalton asked.

"Yes, the woman who left the same day."

"Where is Salina from?"

"I believe her home is a farm near a small village north of here. Her brother came to visit last week, but she did not leave with him." Raylin looked sad. "Carliss is an extraordinary young woman. I hope you find her."

"I will," he said and turned to mount Chaser, but the woman grabbed the horse's bridle.

She looked forlornly at Dalton. "There's something else you should know."

Dalton cocked his head, waiting for more.

"Carliss came to Varlaken because of you."

Dalton was stunned. "What do you mean by that?" he asked.

Raylin hesitated, struggling to find the right words. "I first saw her at Drox's prison, just after you spoke to her. She was bandaging my arm, and I saw a broken heart in her eyes. At first she denied it, but I am able to discern the hearts of people."

Dalton's eyes slowly widened as he considered what Raylin was implying. "I…I had no idea."

Raylin looked sadly at him. "There is no pain greater than that of unreciprocated love."

Unreciprocated love. Dalton felt his own heart lurch. He had been so focused on Brynn that he had never considered anyone else. And yet over the past two weeks he had found himself thinking of Carliss again and again…

Dalton swung into his saddle. "I must go."

"Where will you look?" Raylin asked. "The kingdom is vast."

"If I have to go to the Isles of Sedah and back, I'll find her!" Dalton said.

Raylin nodded and let loose of the bridle. He thanked her and then set his course northeast, pursuing a fellow Knight of the Prince, a friend… and perhaps something more.

There was much to accomplish for the Prince, but in his heart he knew that this mission just might be his greatest.

EPILOGUE

STANDING FIRM

Sir Dalton's journey of knighthood took him into the snares of Lucius and out again. It is a tale I oft tarry to tell yet tell it often, for there are far too many young knights who do not escape the wiles of the Dark Knight. Perhaps by your hearing of it, your heart will be strengthened and your resolve set firm to stay upon the Prince and His ways. It truly is the only way to conquer the evil that casts a shadow upon the hearts of many. Dalton discovered great power to overcome this darkness in the wisdom and instruction of the Prince, for greater is the Prince within than all the powers of Lucius without.

Of Lady Carliss, I should dare to tell of what became of her, and yet her story is one of equal telling and deserves its own chronicle. Whether her chronicle be good or bad I shan't say, for doing so would diminish the purpose for which she strove to live. But in life or in death, you can know that her heart beat strongly for the Prince. She stood firm, and Sir Dalton was inspired by her.

Therefore I leave you with this challenge: stand firm, young knight. Stand firm as Sir Dalton and his faithful friends learned to do, and know that the Prince is with you!

DISCUSSION QUESTIONS

Review Questions for the Kingdom Series

Much of the allegorical symbolism in the Knights of Arrethtrae Series originated in the Kingdom Series. Here are a few questions to review this symbolism:

1. Who does the Prince represent?
2. Who are the Knights of the Prince?
3. Who are the Noble Knights?
4. What is Chessington? Arrethtrae?
5. Who is the Dark Knight/Lucius?
6. Who are the Silent Warriors and the Shadow Warriors?
7. What is a Vincero Knight?
8. What is a haven?

Questions for *Sir Dalton and the Shadow Heart*

CHAPTER 1

1. Drox tells Dalton that he loves to kill incompetent Knights of the Prince. According to 1 Peter 5:8, who is the enemy who is seeking to destroy Christians?
2. Drox exclaims that whoever has the power to kill you is the one who is lord in your life. Do you agree with this statement? Find a Bible verse to support your answer.
3. Why was Dalton unable to defend himself against Drox? If you were faced with a problem like the one Drox represents, how would you use your sword (the Word of God) to combat it?
4. The Bible says that Satan is the "father of lies" (John 8:44, NASB). One of those lies is trying to make people believe that God doesn't really care about them. What are some ways that

you have experienced God's love in your life? Find a few Bible verses that show how much God loves and values you.

CHAPTER 2

1. As Sir Treffen is introducing Sir Dornan to the knights-in-training at the haven, he tells them that Sir Dornan will be their source of instruction and guidance. Who/what should you look to as your primary source of instruction and guidance?
2. All of the trainees at the haven seem to like Sir Dornan's instruction except Koen and Carliss. Why do you think that is?
3. The trainees at the haven make fun of Koen and Carliss for being too serious about their devotion to the Prince and to the Code. Have you ever been teased for being serious about your relationship with God?
4. Sir Dornan claims that he became a Knight of the Prince only after he had undergone training. Does this view line up with the message of Scripture? Use a Bible verse to explain your answer.
5. Sir Dornan claims that the Code is an antiquated guide, not a mandate, and that it is too archaic to apply to the present world. Do you agree? Why or why not? Use Scripture to support your answer.

CHAPTER 3

1. Dalton was unprepared to explain about the Prince to the boy at the water bucket. The Bible says that we are always to be ready to give an answer for what we believe. Read 1 Peter 3:15 and 2 Timothy 4:2. Using Bible verses, how would you explain to someone about Jesus?
2. Each book in the Knights of Arrethtrae Series deals with a specific set of virtues and vices. Can you identify which vices are represented by the boy at the water bucket?

Chapter 4

1. Dalton's encounter with the young man in the city of Millvale is the second phase of doubt, each time growing larger and stronger. How does doubt grow? What does the Bible say about doubt? What can we do to overcome doubt?
2. Satan often uses ridicule or criticism to bring doubt and unbelief into our lives. Have you ever been ridiculed for your faith in Jesus? How did you handle the situation? What attitude does the Bible teach us to have in those situations? Read Matthew 5:11.

Chapter 5

1. Sir Dornan explains to the knights-in-training that because of the great chaos in the Kingdom, it is logical to conclude that the King has removed His influence and involvement from the people of Arrethtrae. What type of view of God is this called? What verses in the Bible counter this philosophy?
2. The attack of the marauders on the village is symbolic of Satan's true intentions for humankind in the world. What are some of the ways he brings devastation to the lives of people? What are some of the ways Jesus brings healing and protection?

Chapter 6

1. In chapter 6, Dalton is faced with the third phase of doubt, and it comes upon him much more strongly than before. Why?
2. Each wound Dalton receives from the harbingers of doubt is deeper than the one before. The wounds are the hurt foot from the bucket, the cut on his leg from the man in Millvale, and the wound to his shoulder from the battle with the warrior. What do these wounds represent spiritually?
3. Why could Koen defeat the warrior when Dalton could not?
4. Koen demonstrates the virtue focused on in this book. What is that virtue? Can you find a Bible verse that defines it?

Chapter 7

1. Dalton is attacked in spite of all of his advanced training. Is it possible for a person to receive great biblical training and still not have faith in Christ? Which group in the Bible had this problem?
2. Lord Drox identifies himself as Skia Ek Distazo, which means "shadow of doubt." Dalton's doubt is now huge and impossible for him to overcome on his own. How or why did this happen? What does this mean in a spiritual sense?
3. Why did Drox fear Koen, yet have control over Dalton?

Chapter 8

1. Who do you think the dark lord represents?
2. Si Kon tells Dalton that it is fear that imprisons them—not the iron bars. Is this true in your life? What do you think hinders believers from sharing the good news of Jesus with everyone they meet? Find a Bible verse that might encourage someone who is dealing with fear in his or her life.

Chapter 9

1. The prisoners of Distazo were discouraged from talking among themselves, and this eliminated any camaraderie or unity. Can you think of an example in our world today of how Satan has deceived Christians and discouraged them from being unified?
2. Drox exclaims to the prisoners of Distazo, "Let he who is strong and not a fool come forth and profess these truths, and I will set him free." Why is this a lie? Find a Bible verse about Satan being a liar.

Chapter 10

1. After Dalton escapes Distazo, seeing evidence of the demise of others causes doubt and unbelief to rise up in him. How does

Satan use what we see, hear, and think about to cause doubt and unbelief in our lives? Find a verse in Philippians that tells us what to think upon.

Chapter 11

1. As Dalton is drifting in and out of consciousness, he hears Mister Sejus singing. Can you find the Scripture verses he is singing?
2. Mister Sejus makes the comment that as a collector he can "take old things and make them new." Can you find a Bible verse that compares our old, sinful nature to that of the new, righteous nature we receive when we are in Christ? What happens to our old nature when we receive the new one?

Chapter 12

1. When Dalton is asked what is most important to him, the first thing he mentions is Lady Brynn. What should be most important to Dalton as a Knight of the Prince? What are the priorities in your life?
2. According to Mister Sejus, why did Dalton's sword break? Can the Word of God ever "break" when one misuses it?
3. Mister Sejus tells Dalton that he has the sword and the mind of a Knight of the Prince, yet he lacks the heart. What does this mean spiritually?
4. After talking with Mister Sejus about the condition of his heart, Dalton "felt pierced again, but this time in his heart and with a different sword." Can you find a verse in Hebrews that talks about the Word of God piercing the reader with truth?

Chapter 13

1. How does the sword that Mister Sejus retrieves from the pile of rubble represent Dalton's condition as a knight and his understanding of the Code?

2. Mister Sejus instructs Dalton to polish the sword according to the designs of its swordsmith. How does this apply to how we read and understand the Bible?
3. Dalton says that many people in the kingdom deny the existence of the King. Sejus replies that those people live a life of contradiction because even the kingdom itself testifies to the King's reign. Does this statement apply to our world today? How? Find a Bible verse to support your answer.
4. One of Satan's most successful lies of all time is that of evolution. Why do you suppose he chose to convince people to believe in evolution, and why is it so successful in destroying people's faith?
5. What does Nedehaven represent?

CHAPTER 14

1. Dalton was under the false belief that it was training from instructors that directed the thoughts and actions of Knights of the Prince. Mister Sejus guides him to the truth that it should be the Code and the life of the Prince that direct the thoughts and actions of a Knight of the Prince. What does this represent, and why is it important for us to understand?
2. Find a verse in John that relates to the Prince's being the personification of the Code.
3. Who does Master Sejus represent? What is the significance of Dalton finally addressing Sejus as *Master* rather than *Mister*?

CHAPTER 15

1. Master Sejus says, "Even the treasures of a king are oft neglected, but it does not diminish their value." What do these words refer to in a spiritual sense?
2. Master Sejus gives Dalton's life and the sword to him as gifts. How has Jesus done the same for us? List a couple of Bible verses to support your answer.

3. Dalton believed Sejus to be different than He really was. Dalton's perception of Sejus changes the more he gets to know Him. How can we know who Jesus really is? How does our perception of the Lord affect our relationship with Him?
4. Dalton has come to the realization that the Prince is the "cornerstone" of all Master Sejus has taught him. Find a Bible verse referring to Jesus as the cornerstone.
5. To what is Sejus referring when He tells Dalton that He will be in Dalton forever and Dalton will be in Sejus forever? Find a passage of Scripture that explains this.
6. Just before Dalton and Sejus part ways, Sejus reminds him, "Dalton, I came to you because you called for me." What does this represent? Use Romans 10:13 to support your answer.

CHAPTER 16

1. Why do you think that talking so much about the Prince brought tension to Dalton's relationship with Lady Brynn? Have you ever experienced tension in a relationship because of your strong faith in Christ?

CHAPTER 17

1. What do the death ravens represent according to Matthew 13:4, 19 and Ephesians 6:16?

CHAPTER 18

1. When Dalton encounters Drox on his return to the prison of Distazo (doubt), he tells Drox that he (Drox) feeds on the fears of others and that he has no real power over any of the knights he holds prisoner. If this is true, where does Drox's power come from?

2. Has there ever been a time in your life when you have determined to pursue God wholeheartedly or encouraged others to follow Him? Does it seem that the devil attacks more fiercely at those times? Why or why not?

Chapter 19

1. Dalton was encouraged to find that Koen and Carliss had joined him in the battle against Drox and the Vincero Knights. Have you ever gone to battle against the powers of darkness for a friend or had a friend go to battle for you? How might you do this?

Chapter 20

1. After the prisoners were released from Distazo, some refused to leave out of fear of Drox's threats. Can you find a verse in Galatians that encourages believers to live in freedom and not in bondage?
2. Christ has equipped and commissioned you to the same call as that of Sir Dalton—to free prisoners from darkness. Can you find a passage in Isaiah that confirms this truth?

Chapter 21

1. When Koen becomes concerned about Carliss's disappearance, Dalton and Orland offer to help in any way possible. They are true friends to Koen. Read Proverbs 18:24. What might produce such a close friendship?
2. Review the virtue and the vice or stronghold this book focuses on. Can you name them?

ANSWERS TO DISCUSSION QUESTIONS

Answers for the Kingdom Series

1. The Prince represents Jesus Christ.
2. The Knights of the Prince represent all Christians.
3. The Noble Knights represent the Jews who were hostile to Jesus and His disciples (the Pharisees, for example).
4. Chessington represents Jerusalem, and Arrethtrae represents the whole world (*earth* and *terra* are combined backward to make up this word).
5. The Dark Knight, also referred to as Lucius, represents Satan.
6. The Silent Warriors are God's angels, and the Shadow Warriors are Satan's demons.
7. A Vincero Knight is a person who has been personally trained by one of Lucius's Shadow Warriors to spread and cultivate evil. Vincero Knights are ruthless and twisted by the evil that has mentored them. They represent people who are committed to propagating evil in the world, such as murderers, drug dealers, and the like.
8. A haven represents a local church, where believers are trained, discipled, and sent out to share the gospel with others.

Answers for *Sir Dalton and the Shadow Heart*

Chapter 1

1. 1 Peter 5:8 says, "Be sober, be vigilant; because your adversary the devil walks about like a roaring lion, seeking whom he may devour." Our enemy is the devil and his demons. Lord Drox represents one of Satan's demons.

2. Jesus says in Luke 12:4, "And I say to you, My friends, do not be afraid of those who kill the body, and after that have no more that they can do." Having the power to kill another person does not make anyone lord. Many believers have been martyred for their faith in Jesus, but those who murdered them could not rob them of the eternal life they have in Christ Jesus.
3. Dalton didn't know how to use his sword to defeat Drox. He had been depending on his own strength instead of relying on the power of the Prince. True power comes from God's Holy Word, so it is important to memorize Scripture to be ready for battle against Satan and his fallen angels.
4. Answers based on personal experience. Some examples are Psalm 139; John 3:16; and 1 John 4:9–10.

Chapter 2

1. According to 2 Timothy 3:16, the Bible should be our primary source of instruction and guidance. It reads, "All Scripture is given by inspiration of God, and is profitable for doctrine, for reproof, for correction, for instruction in righteousness."
2. Read 2 Timothy 4:3–4. Koen and Carliss know that Sir Dornan's teaching is contrary to the teachings of the Prince. The only way to identify false teachers is to first know the truth of the Word. The other trainees are more comfortable listening to a teacher who only tells them what they want to hear.
3. Answers based on personal experience.
4. The Bible says in Ephesians 2:8–9 that we are saved by God's free gift of grace, not by our own works.
5. John 1:1 states that "the Word was God." We know that God lives and reigns forever. So also His Word lives and reigns forever as it says in Matthew 24:35: "Heaven and earth will pass away, but My words will by no means pass away." The Bible is as applicable to us today as when it was written.

Chapter 3

1. Answers will vary. Some supporting verses are: Mark 14:61–62; John 14:6; John 18:36–37; 1 Corinthians 15:3–4; and Revelation 1:18.
2. The vices of doubt and unbelief surface in Dalton when he encounters the boy at the water bucket. Doubt can start out small and seemingly harmless, but it often grows into a stronghold if it is not confronted with the truth of the Word of God. It is normal for people to have questions about their faith from time to time, but God's Word is strong enough to answer those questions. Asking honest questions, in fact, can actually be a sign of faith. The vice of doubt is more a matter of allowing oneself to sink into despair or cynicism instead of trusting God with questions.

Chapter 4

1. Doubt grows when it is not confronted with the truth of Christ. Jesus says in Luke 8:50, "Do not be afraid; only believe" (see also Matthew 21:21–22). The only way to overcome doubt is to put your faith in the Word of God rather than in what you see, hear, taste, smell, or feel (1 John 5:4).
2. Answers based on personal experience. You are blessed when you receive persecution or ridicule for Christ's sake. Romans 12:21 reminds us not to be overcome by evil, but to overcome evil with good.

Chapter 5

1. This view of God is called deism. Deism is the belief that a supreme God exists and created the universe but does not interact or intervene in the affairs of human life or the natural laws of the universe. Some verses to counter this philosophy are Matthew 28:20; John 17:9–26; and Hebrews 13:5–6.

2. Some examples of Satan's devastation are depression, blaming God when bad things happen, pride, adultery, rebellion, greed, and doubt. Jesus brings healing and protection through *love,* encouragement from other believers, provision of every need, the comfort and guidance of the Holy Spirit, and the wisdom of the Bible.

CHAPTER 6

1. Doubt is stronger here because Dalton has chosen to tolerate and even entertain doubt rather than rebuke it with the truth of who the Prince is and what the Prince did for Dalton.
2. These wounds represent wounds to our faith. If doubt isn't dealt with biblically, it can hinder and even cripple our faith.
3. Koen is able to defeat the warrior because he operates in his identity as a Knight of the Prince and because the Prince bestows His power and authority upon those who follow Him. This represents the power and authority given to us by Jesus. Read Mark 16:15–20.
4. Koen demonstrates the virtue of faith, which is the opposite of the vice of doubt. The Bible defines faith in Hebrews 11:1 as "the substance of things hoped for, the evidence of things not seen."

CHAPTER 7

1. The Pharisees and Sadducees had ample head knowledge of Scripture but did not believe it in their hearts. They couldn't recognize Jesus for who He was, even when He was standing right in front of them.
2. Dalton has yet to confront doubt with the truth that because he wields the power of the Prince, Dalton is stronger than

doubt. Until you know who you are in Christ and what you have because of Christ, you are ineffective in the spiritual battle against the powers of darkness in the world. Read 1 John 4:13, 17–18.

3. Drox knew that he had no power over Koen. The only power that Drox had was given to him by Dalton. Likewise, the only power that Satan and his demons have over a child of God is that which a believer gives them. When Jesus died for our sins on the cross, He stripped Satan and his demons of their power (Colossians 2:14–15; Hebrews 2:14). Sometimes Christians forget this.

CHAPTER 8

1. The dark lord represents Satan—or in the world of Arrethtrae, Lucius.
2. Answers based on personal experience. Both fear and doubt can hinder a believer from sharing the gospel. Examples are 1 John 4:16–19 and 2 Timothy 1:7.

CHAPTER 9

1. Answers based on personal experience.
2. Jesus says *His* truth will set you free (John 8:32). In reality, not believing in the Lord's truth puts people in a prison run by Satan. Only faith in Christ can free us. One example is John 8:44.

CHAPTER 10

1. Some ways that we let doubt and unbelief into our lives are through the media (movies, television, books, etc.) and demoralizing conversation. If we choose to engage in unwholesome activities and dwell on unwholesome thoughts, we give strength to doubt and unbelief. Read Philippians 4:8.

CHAPTER 11

1. Proverbs 12:15, 19.
2. Second Corinthians 5:17. This verse tells us that our old nature has passed away. When a person dies, sometimes we say that he has passed away, as in he is dead and cannot exist any longer on this earth. It is the same with our old, sinful nature. When we begin a relationship with Christ, we receive a new nature, and our old nature dies and is gone forever. Our new nature does not exist in addition to our old nature but instead replaces our old nature.

CHAPTER 12

1. Dalton's commitment to the Prince should be the most important thing in his life. Likewise in our lives, our relationship with Jesus should be our first priority. Read Matthew 6:33 and Matthew 22:37–38.
2. Mister Sejus explains that the sword could only break if it were used by one who lacked the proper skill. God's Word can never actually "break." However, it can be misinterpreted or misrepresented by people who do not have the Holy Spirit to guide their understanding, who have limited knowledge or maturity in its application, or who have ulterior motives.
3. Dalton was simply going through the motions of being a Knight of the Prince, but he lacked the heart or the passion to truly follow Him. In Revelation 3:16, Jesus warns the Laodiceans that they have become lukewarm in their Christian walk. They did not have the true heart of a believer.
4. Hebrews 4:12.

CHAPTER 13

1. To be effective in battle, a sword must be polished and sharpened beforehand. The rusted and dull sword represents the

spiritual condition of a believer who has not studied and memorized God's Word in preparation for battle against Satan (see 2 Timothy 2:15). Dalton did not practice the Code or apply it to his life.

2. We must be sure that we understand the Bible as God intended and not base our understanding completely on the ideas and opinions of others. This doesn't mean we shouldn't seek guidance and teaching, just that we need to study God's Word diligently for ourselves and ask for the Holy Spirit's guidance.
3. This applies more today than ever before. The theory of evolution has been embraced by most of the world and is an attempt to deny the existence of God. Creation itself testifies to the existence of a Creator. Some examples are Psalm 19:1–3; Job 12:7–10; Romans 1:20.
4. Genesis is the foundation of Christianity. Without the solid truth of Genesis, there is no God and no need for a Savior. Therefore, Satan uses evolution to attack the foundation of our faith. The complexity of even a single-celled organism is far greater than anything man has created, and yet a person would be considered a lunatic if he or she believed that a digital watch found in the wilderness evolved into its current form of functionality. The Bible tells us in Romans 1:22 that such people, "professing to be wise, [become] fools." There are some excellent scientific creationist organizations that have been established to counter Satan's great lie.
5. Eden (N-E-D-E haven).

Chapter 14

1. Just as the Code and the life of the Prince should direct the thoughts and the actions of a Knight of the Prince, so the Bible and the life of Christ should direct the thoughts and actions of

Christians. It is important that we believers are constantly in the Word so we can discern and verify those things being taught.

2. John 1:1.
3. Jesus (S-E-J-U-S). Dalton finally recognizes the lordship of Sejus. Similarly, once a person truly understands who Jesus is and what He has done for humankind on the cross, he or she is humbled…and Jesus can then become Lord to them.

CHAPTER 15

1. The treasures of God—such as forgiveness, mercy, and salvation—are cast aside by most of the human race. However, this does not diminish the value of these incredible treasures, especially for those who understand and accept them.
2. Jesus gave us the gift of eternal life (Ephesians 2:8–9). He also gave us the Bible to instruct and guide us (2 Timothy 3:16) and for us to use in the battle against the powers of darkness in this world (Ephesians 6:10–17).
3. Sejus's transformation from a weak old man to a strong man of great power and wisdom represents the transformation that occurs in the mind of a person who begins to understand who Jesus really is. An unbeliever often gives little regard or respect to Jesus and will even take His name in vain, but once a person is saved, his or her mind is enlightened to the glory and power of Jesus. We know who God really is by reading His Word and by communicating with Him in prayer. Our perception of who God is can greatly affect our relationship with Him in that we limit what He can do in our lives by what we believe He is capable of.
4. Some examples are Matthew 21:42; Ephesians 2:20; and 1 Peter 2:6.

5. Dalton represents a person who has a new life in Christ, just as Christ is in him. John 15:1–7 explains this.
6. When we call on Jesus, He promises to save us. Romans 10:13 says, "Whoever calls on the name of the LORD shall be saved."

CHAPTER 16

1. Sometimes a believer's strong faith may accentuate the rift that exists when two people do not share a similar bond in Christ. A believer who is completely "sold out" for Christ can often cause lukewarm Christians to feel uncomfortable. Answers based on personal experience.

CHAPTER 17

1. The death ravens represent the evil works of Satan that aim to "devour" or destroy truth and faith like the birds who devoured the seed in Jesus' parable. They are the fiery darts mentioned in Ephesians 6:16 that can only be quenched by the shield of faith.

CHAPTER 18

1. The only power Drox has is given to him by those who submit themselves to fear and doubt. As a Knight of the Prince and as a child of God, you have not been given "a spirit of fear, but of power and of love and of a sound mind" (2 Timothy 1:7).
2. When we pursue God wholeheartedly, we move to the front line of the spiritual battle to expand the kingdom of God. This is where the great rewards are won and can also be where we are buffeted by Satan, just as Paul was (see 2 Corinthians 12:7). Although we are attacked, remember that 1 John 4:4 states, "He who is in you is greater than he who is in the world." Rest of answer based on personal experience.

Chapter 19

1. Answers based on personal experience. Prayer is one of our greatest weapons against evil, for through prayer we have direct access to the incredible power of God. Christian fellowship and edification (building up) are also a powerful help for those facing spiritual battles. Dalton would not have been able to defeat Lord Drox without the fellowship and support of Koen, Carliss, and Si Kon.

Chapter 20

1. Galatians 5:1.
2. Two possibilities are Isaiah 61:1–3 and Isaiah 42:6–7.

Chapter 21

1. Proverbs 18:24 says, "A man who has friends must himself be friendly, but there is a friend who sticks closer than a brother." Enduring an extreme hardship together, such as a fierce battle, can forge such a tight, close, loving, and loyal relationship—one that transcends even family bonds. This can easily happen with fellow believers in Jesus Christ, for they share the same Holy Spirit and are in the ultimate battle between Good and Evil. Sharing this experience can indeed create a friend that is closer than a brother (or sister).
2. The virtue of faith and the vice or stronghold of doubt.

The Shadow Heart

cresc.

ff maestoso

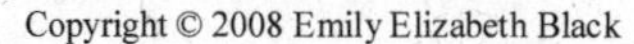

mf
cresc.
8vb
ritard.
ff

AUTHOR COMMENTARY

Young people today face an entire arsenal of fiery weapons that Satan casts at them. Without diligent biblical teaching and true relationship with Jesus, there is no foundation for them to stand upon. It is easy to see why so many lose their way as they leave home. This is a travesty, for God has given all evidence and power to equip our young people to stand strong.

Hebrews 11:6 tells us that without faith it is impossible to please God. It is paramount that we give our young people every opportunity to increase their faith so that they may stand against shadows of doubt that will come their way. Satan placed the seeds of doubt in Eve's mind, and a paradise was lost because of it. My passion, as conveyed through *Sir Dalton and the Shadow Heart,* is to reveal the dangers of allowing doubt and unbelief to become a stronghold in the heart of a young person and to encourage him or her to strengthen faith through the overwhelming evidence in creation, Scripture, and changed lives.

> *Take heed, brethren, lest there be in any of you an evil heart of unbelief, in departing from the living God.*
>
> —HEBREWS 3:12, KJV

> *So Jesus answered and said to them, "Have faith in God. For assuredly, I say to you, whoever says to this mountain, 'Be removed and be cast into the sea,' and does not doubt in his heart, but believes that those things he says will be done, he will have whatever he says. Therefore I say to you, whatever things you ask when you pray, believe that you receive them, and you will have them."*
>
> —MARK 11:22–24